John Bloundelle

The Silent Shore

outlook

John Bloundelle-Burton

The Silent Shore

1st Edition | ISBN: 978-3-75234-853-8

Place of Publication: Frankfurt am Main, Germany

Year of Publication: 2020

Outlook Verlag GmbH, Germany.

Reproduction of the original.

THE SILENT SHORE

BY

JNO. BLOUNDELLE-BURTON

Prologue

THE STORY OF THIRTY YEARS AGO

"And you are certain of the year he was married in?"

"Perfectly—there is no possibility of my being mistaken. He was married on New Year's Day, '58; I was born in May, '59."

"It is strange, certainly. But there is one solution of it—is it not possible that, even if this is he, the lady registered as his wife might not have been so? In fact she could not have been, otherwise he could never have married your mother."

"I will not believe it! He was too cold and austere—too puritanical I had almost said—to form any such connection."

"Do you think, then, that he would commit bigamy?"

"I don't know what to think!" the other answered gloomily.

Two men, both about the same age, twenty-five, were seated in a private room at an inn, known as the Hôtel Bellevue, at Le Vocq, a dreary fishing town with a good though small harbour, a dozen miles west of Havre. On a fine day the bay that runs in from Barfleur to Fécamp is gay and bright, but it presented a melancholy appearance on this occasion, as the two young men gazed out at it across the rain-soaked plots of grass that formed the lawn of the "Bellevue." Down below the cliff on which the inn stood, the port was visible, and in the port was to be seen an English cutter, the *Electra*, in which the friends had run for Le Vocq when the storm, that had now been raging for twenty-four hours, broke upon them. They had left Cowes a fortnight ago, and had been yachting pleasantly in the Channel since, putting into Cherbourg on one occasion, into Ste. Mère Eglise on another, and Havre on a third; and now, as ill-luck would have it, it seemed as if they were doomed to be weather-bound in, of the many dreary places on the coast, the dreariest of all, Le Vocq.

The first night in the inn, to which they had come up after seeing the yacht made snug and comfortable in the harbour below, and the sailors left in charge of her also provided for, passed easily enough. There was the hope of the storm abating—which was cheering—and they had cards, and some Paris newspapers to read, and above all, they were fatigued and could sleep well.

2

But, on the next day, the storm had not abated, and they were tired of cards, the old Paris papers had been read and re-read, and later ones had not arrived, and they were refreshed with their night's rest and wanted to be off. But there was no getting off, and what was to be done?

They had stood all the morning looking out of the window disconsolately, had smoked pipes and cigarettes innumerable, and had yawned a good deal, and sworn a little.

"What the deuce are we to do to prevent ourselves from dying of *ennui*, Philip?" the one asked the other.

"Jerry," the other answered solemnly, "I know no more than you do. There is nothing left to read, and soon—very soon, alas!—there will be nothing left to smoke but the *caporal* obtainable in the village. That, however, might poison us and end our miseries."

Then the one called Philip began looking about the salon that was at their disposal, and whistling plaintively, and peering into the cupboards, of which there were two:

"Hullo!" he suddenly exclaimed, "here is another great mental treat for us —a lot of old books; and precious big ones, too! I wonder what they are?"

"Pull them out and let us see. Probably only *Le Monde Illustré*, or *Le Journal Amusant*, bound up for the landlord's winter nights' delectation, after they have been thumbed by every sailor in the village."

"Oh, confound the books!" Philip exclaimed when he had looked into them, "they are only the old registers, the *Livres des Étrangers* of bygone years."

"Nevertheless, let us see them," the other answered; "at any rate we shall learn what kind of company the house has kept."

So, obeying his behest, Philip brought them out, and they sat down "to begin at the beginning," as they said laughingly; and each took a volume and commenced to peruse it.

Every now and then they told one another of some name they had come across, the owner of which was known to them by hearsay, and they agreed that the "Hôtel Bellevue" had, in its day, had some very good people for its guests. They had found several titles—English—inscribed in the pages of the register, and also many prominent names belonging to the same nationality.

"Probably half these people have occupied this very sitting-room at some time or the other," Philip said to Gervase. "I only wish to heaven some of them were here now, and that—"

3

He stopped at a sudden exclamation of his friend, who was gazing fixedly at the page before him.

"What kind of a find is it now, Jerry?" he asked. "Any one very wonderful?"

"It must be a mistake," the other said in a low voice. "And yet how could such a mistake happen? Look at this!" and he pointed with his finger to a line in the book.

"By Jove!" the other exclaimed, as he read, "*Août* 17, 1854, *L'Hon. Gervase Occleve et sa femme.*" Then he said, "Your father of course, before he inherited his title?"

"Of course! There never was any other Gervase Occleve in existence, except myself, while he was alive. But what can it mean?"

"It means that your father knew this place many years ago, and came here: that is all, I should say. It is a coincidence, but after all it is no more strange that he should know Le Vocq, than that you should."

"But you don't see the curious part of it, Philip! It is the words *et sa femme*. My father had no wife in 1854! He never had a wife until he married my mother, and then he was Lord Penlyn and no longer known as Gervase Occleve."

And then followed the conversation with which this story opens.

"It *is* a strange thing," Philip said, "but it must be a mistake."

In his own heart, being somewhat of a worldling, he did not think it was any mistake at all. He thought it highly probable that the late Lord Penlyn had, when here, a lady travelling with him who was registered as his wife, but who, in actual fact, was not his wife at all.

After a few moments spent in thought, Gervase turned to his friend and said, "The landlord, the man who stared so hard at me yesterday when we came in, was an elderly person. He may have had this hotel in '54, might even remember this mysterious namesake of mine. I think I will ask him to come up."

"I shouldn't," Philip said. "He isn't at all likely to remember anything about it." In his mind he thought it very probable that the man might, even at that distance of time, remember something of Gervase's father, especially if he had made a long stay at the house, and would perhaps be able to give some reminiscences of his whilom guest that might by no means make his son feel comfortable.

But his remonstrance was unheeded, and the other rang the bell. It was answered by a tidy waitress wearing the cap peculiar to the district, to whom Gervase—who was an excellent linguist—said in very good French:

"If the landlord is in, will you be good enough to say that Lord Penlyn would be glad to speak to him?"

The girl withdrew, and in a few minutes the landlord tapped at the door. When he had received an invitation to enter, he came into the room and bowed respectfully, but, as he did so, Lord Penlyn again noticed that his eyes were fixed upon him with a wondering stare; a stare exactly the same as he had received on the previous day when they entered the hotel. There was nothing rude nor offensive in the look; it partook more of the nature of an incredulous gaze than anything else.

"Milor has expressed a wish to see me," he said as he entered. "He has, I trust, found everything to his wish in my poor house!"

"Perfectly," Gervase answered; "but I want to ask you a question. Will you be seated?" And then when the landlord had taken a chair—still looking intently at him—he went on:

"We found these *Livres des Étrangers* in your cupboard, and, for want of anything else to read, we took them down and have been amusing ourselves with them. I hope we did not take a liberty."

"*Mais, Milor!*" the landlord said with a shrug of his shoulders and a twitch of his eyebrows, that were meant to express his satisfaction at his guests being able to find anything to distract them.

"Thank you," Gervase said. "Well! in going through this book—the one of 1854—I have come upon a name so familiar to me, the name of Gervase Occleve, that—"

But before he could finish his sentence the landlord had jumped up from his chair, and was speaking rapidly while he gesticulated in a thorough French fashion.

"*C'est ça, mon Dieu, mais oui!*" he began. "Occleve—of course! That is the face. Sir, Milor! I salute you! When you entered my house yesterday, I said to myself, 'But where, mon Dieu, but where have I seen him? Or is it but the spirit of some dead one looking at me out of his eyes?' And now that you mention to me the name of Occleve, then in a moment he comes back to me and I see him once again. *Ah! ma foi, Milor!* but when I regard you, then in verity he returns to me, and I recall him as he used to sit in this very room —*parbleu!* in that very chair in which you now sit."

The young men had both stared at him with some amazement as he spoke

5

hurriedly and excitedly, repeating himself in his earnestness, and now as he ceased, Gervase said:

"Do I understand you to say, then, that I bear such a likeness to this man, whose name is inscribed here, as to recall him vividly to you?" "*Mais, sans doute!* you are his son! It must be so. There is only one thing that I do not comprehend. You bear a different name."

"He became Lord Penlyn later in life, and at his death that title came to me."

"*Bien compris!* And so he is dead! He can scarcely have lived the full space of man's years. And Madame your mother? She is well?"

For a moment the young man hesitated. Then he said: "She is dead too."

"*Pauvre dame,*" the landlord said, and as he spoke it seemed as though he was talking to himself. "She was bright and happy in those days so far off, bright and happy once; and she, too, is gone. And I, who was older than either of them, am left! But, Lord Penlyn," he said, readdressing himself to his guest, "you look younger than your years. It is thirty years since you used to run about those sands outside and play; I have carried you to them often—"

"You carried me to those sands thirty years ago! Why, I was not—"

"Stop!" Philip Smerdon said to him in English, and speaking in a low tone. "Do you not see it all? Say no more."

"Yes," Gervase answered. "Yes, I see it all."

Later on, when the landlord had left the room after insisting upon shaking the hand of "the child he had known thirty years ago," Gervase said:

"So he who was so stern and self-contained, who seemed to be above the ordinary weaknesses of other men, was, after all, worse than the majority of them. I suppose he flung this poor woman off when he married my mother, I suppose he left the boy, for whom this man takes me—to starve or to become a thief preying on his fellow men. It is not pleasant to think that I have an elder brother who may be an outcast, perhaps a felon!"

"I should not take quite such a pessimist view of things as that," Philip said. "For aught you know, the lady he had with him here may have died between 1854 and 1858, and, for the matter of that, so may the boy; or he may have made a good allowance to both when he parted with them. For anything you know to the contrary he might have seen the boy frequently until his death, and have taken care to place him comfortably in the world."

"In such a case I must have known it. I must have met him somewhere."

"Nothing more unlikely! The world is large enough—in spite of the numerous jokes about its smallness—for two peculiarly situated individuals not to meet. If I were you, Jerry, I should think no more about the matter."

"It is not a thing one can easily forget!" the other answered.

The landlord had given them a description of what he remembered of the Gervase Occleve whom he had known thirty years ago, but what he had told them had not thrown much light upon the subject. He described how Gervase Occleve had first come there in the summer of '54 accompanied by his wife (he evidently had never doubted that they were married) and by his son, "the Monsieur now before him," as he said innocently. They had lived very quietly, occupying the very rooms in which they were now sitting, he told the young men; roaming about the sands in the day, or driving over to the adjacent towns and villages, or sailing in a boat that Mr. Occleve hired by the month. They seemed contented and happy enough, he said, and stayed on and on until the autumn's damp and rain, peculiar to that part of the coast, drove them away. It was strange, he thought, that Milor did not remember anything about that period; but it was true, he was but a little child!

Then, he continued, in the following summer they returned again, and again spent some months there—and then, he never saw nor heard of them more. But, so well did he remember Mr. Occleve's face, even after all these years, that, ever since Lord Penlyn had been in the house, he had been puzzling his brains to think where he had seen him before. He certainly should not, he said, have remembered the child he had played with so often, but that his likeness to his father was more than striking. To Madame, his mother, he saw no resemblance at all.

"But I did not tell him," he said to himself afterwards, as he sat in his parlour below and sipped a little red wine meditatively, "I did not tell him that on the second summer a gloom had fallen over them, and that I often saw her in tears, and heard him speak harshly to her. Why should I? À quoi bon to disturb the poor young man's meditations on his dead father and mother!"

And the good landlord went out and served a chopine of *petit bleu* to one customer, and a *tasse* of *absinthe gommée* to another, and entertained them with an account of how there was, upstairs, an English Milor who had been there thirty years ago with his father; the Milor who was the owner of the yacht now in port.

On the next day the storm was over, there was almost a due south wind, and the *Electra* was skimming over the waves and leaving the dreary French coast far behind it.

"It hasn't been a pleasant visit," Lord Penlyn said to Philip, as they leant

7

over the bows smoking their pipes and watching Le Vocq fade gradually into a speck. "I would give something never to have heard that story!"

"It is the story of thirty years ago," his friend answered. "And it is not you who did the wrong. Why let it worry you?"

"I cannot help it! And—I daresay you will think me a fool!—but I cannot also help wondering on which of my father's children—upon that other nameless and unknown one, or upon me—his sins will be visited!"

The Story

CHAPTER I.

Ida Raughton sat, on a bright June day of that year, in her pretty boudoir looking out on the well-kept gardens of a West End square, and thinking of an important event in her life that was now not very far off—her marriage. Within the last month she had become engaged, not without some earlier doubts on her part as to whether she was altogether certain of her feelings— though, afterwards, she told herself over and over again that the man to whom she was now promised was the only one she could ever love: and the wedding-day was fixed for the 1st of September. Her future husband was Gervase Occleve, Viscount Penlyn.

She was the only daughter of Sir Paul Raughton, a wealthy Surrey baronet, and had been to him, since her mother's death, as the apple of his eye—the only thing that to him seemed to make life worth living. It was true that he had distractions that are not uncommon to elderly gentlemen of means, and possessed of worldly tastes; perfectly true that Paris and Nice, and Ascot and Newmarket, as well as his clubs and his friends—not always male ones—had charms for him that were still very seductive; but, after all, they were nothing in comparison to his daughter's love and his love for her. Never during his long widowerhood, a widowerhood dating from her infancy, had he failed to make her life and happiness the central object of his existence; never had he allowed his pleasures to stand in the way of the study of her comfort. The best schools and masters when she was a child, the best friends and chaperons for her when womanhood was approaching, and when it had arrived, the greatest liberality as regards cheques for dressmakers, milliners, upholsterers, horses, etc., had been but a small part of his way of showing his devotion to her. And she had returned his affection, had been to him a daughter giving back love for love, and endeavouring in every way in her power to make him an ample return for all the thought and care he had showered on her. Of course he had foreseen that the inevitable day must come when—love him however much she might—she would still be willing to leave him, when she would be willing to resign being mistress of her father's house to be mistress of her husband's. His worldly knowledge, which was extensive enough for half-a-dozen ordinary men, told him clearly enough that the parent nest very soon palled on the bird that saw its way to building one for itself. Yet, when the blow fell, as he had known it must fall, he did not find that his philosophy enabled him to endure it very lightly. On the other hand, there was his love for her, and that bade him let her go, since it was for her happiness that she should do so.

"I promised her mother when she lay dying," he said to himself, "that my life should be devoted to her, and I have kept my vow to the best of my power. I am not going to break it now. Besides, it is part of a father's duty to see his daughter well married; and I suppose Penlyn is a good match. At any rate, there are plenty of other fathers and mothers who would like to have caught him for their girls."

That she should have made a sensation during her first season was not a thing to astonish Sir Paul, nor, indeed, any one else. Ida Raughton was as thoroughly beautiful a girl, when first she made her appearance in London society, as any who had ever taken their place in its ranks. Tall and graceful, and possessed of an exquisitely shaped head, round which her auburn hair curled in thick locks; with bright hazel eyes, whose expression varied in accordance with their owner's thoughts and feelings, sometimes sparkling with laughter and mirth, and sometimes saddened with tears as she listened to any tale of sorrow; with a nose the line of which was perfect, and a mouth, the smallness of which disguised, though it could not hide, the even, white teeth within, no one could look at Ida without acknowledging how lovely she was. Even other and rival *débutantes* granted her loveliness, and the woman who can obtain such a concession as this from her sisters has fairly established her right to homage.

As she sat at her boudoir window on this June day, thinking of her now

9

definitely settled marriage, she was wondering if the life before her would be as bright and happy as the one she was leaving behind for ever. That—with the exception of the death of her mother, a sorrow that time had mercifully tempered to her—had been without alloy. Would the future be so? There was no reason to think otherwise, she reflected, no reason to doubt it. Lord Penlyn was young, handsome, and manly, the owner of an honoured name, and well endowed with the world's goods. Yet that would not have weighed with her had she not loved him.

She had asked herself if she did love him several times before she consented to give him the answer he desired, and then she acknowledged that he alone had won her heart. She recalled other men's attentions to her, their soft words, their desire to please; how they had haunted her footsteps at balls and at the Opera, and how no other man's homage had ever been so sweet to her as the homage of Gervase Occleve. At first—wishing still to be sure of herself—she would not agree to be his wife, telling him that she did not know her heart; but when he asked her a second time, after she had had ample opportunity for reflection, she told him he should have his wish.

"And you do love me, Ida?" he asked rapturously, perhaps boyishly, as they drove back from a large dinner-party to which they had gone at Richmond. "You are sure you do?"

"Yes," she said, "I am sure I do. I was not sure when first you asked me, but I am now."

"Then kiss me, darling, and tell me so. Otherwise I shall scarcely be able to believe it;" and he bent over her and kissed her, and she returned the kiss.

"I love you, Gervase," she said, blushing as she did so.

"You have made me supremely happy," he said to her after their lips had met; "happy beyond all thought. And, dearest, you shall never have cause to repent of it. I will be to you the best, the truest husband woman ever had. There shall be no shadow ever come over your life that I can keep away."

For answer she put her hand in his, and so they drove along the lanes that were getting thick with hawthorn and chestnut blossom, while ahead of them sounded the merry voices of others of the party who were on a four-in-hand. They had come down, a joyous company, from town in the afternoon, had dined at the "Star and Garter," and were now on their way home under the soft moonlight of an early summer evening. Sir Paul had been with them in the landau on the journey out, but on this return one he was seated on the top of the coach, talking to a lady whom he addressed more than once as "his dear old friend," and was smoking innumerable cigarettes. Probably he did not imagine for one moment that Lord Penlyn was going to take this opportunity of proposing to his daughter; but he had noticed that they seemed to enjoy each other's society very much, especially when they could enjoy it alone. And so, all things being suitable and harmonious, and the baronet having a heart beneath his exceedingly well-fitting waistcoat—and that a very big heart where Ida was concerned—had let them have the gratification of the drive home together.

"And you never loved any other man, Ida?" Gervase asked. "Forgive the question, but every lover likes to know, or think, that no one has ever been before him in the affection of the woman he loves."

"No," she answered, "never. You are the first man I have ever loved."

This had happened nearly a month ago, but as Ida sat in her boudoir her thoughts returned to the drive on that May night. Yes, she acknowledged, she loved him, and she loved him more and more every time she saw him. But as she recalled this conversation she also recalled the question he had asked her, the question as to whether she had ever loved any other man; and she wondered what had made him ask it. Could it be that it was supposed by some of their circle—though erroneously supposed, she told herself—that another man loved her? Perfectly erroneously, because that other man had never breathed one word of love to her; and because, though he would sometimes be in her society continually for perhaps a week, and then be absent for a month, he never, during all the time they were thus constantly meeting, paid her more marked attention than other men were in the habit of doing. Yet, notwithstanding this, it had come to her knowledge that it had been whispered about that Walter Cundall loved her.

This man, Walter Cundall, this reported admirer of hers, was well known in society, was in a way famous, though his fame was in the principal part due to the simplest purchaser of that commodity—to wealth. He was known to be stupendously rich, to be able to spend any large sum of money he chose in order to gratify his inclinations, to be able to look upon thousands as ordinary men looked upon hundreds, and upon hundreds as other men looked upon tens. This was the principal part of his fame; but there was a lesser, though a better part! It was true that he did spend hundreds and thousands, but, as a rule, he spent them quite as much upon others as upon himself. His fours-in-hand, his yachts and steam-yachts, his villa at Cookham, and his house in Grosvenor Place, as well as his villa at Cannes—to which a joyous party went every winter—were as much for his friends as for him. He gave dinners that men and women delighted in getting invitations to; but it was noticed that, though his *chéf* was a marvel, he rarely ate of anything but the soup and joint himself, and that, while others were drinking the best wine that Burgundy, or Aÿ, or Rheims could produce, he scarcely ever quenched his thirst with anything but a tumbler of claret. But he would sit at the head of his table with a smile of satisfaction upon his handsome face, contented with the knowledge that his guests were happy and enjoying themselves.

This man of whom Ida was now thinking and whose story may be told here, had commenced life at Westminster School, to which he had been put by his uncle, a rich owner of mines and woods in Honduras, from which place he paid flying visits to England once a year, or once in two years. The boy was an orphan, left by his mother to her brother's care, and that brother had not failed in his trust. The lad went to Westminster with the full understanding that Honduras must be his home when school days were over; but he knew that it would be a home of luxury and tropical splendour. There, after his school days, he passed some years of his life, attending to the mines, seeing to the consignments of shiploads of mahogany and cedar, going for days in the hills with no companions but the Mestizos and the Indians, and helping his uncle to garner up more and more wealth that was eventually destined to be his. Once or twice in the space of ten years he came to Europe, generally with the object of increasing their connection with London or Continental cities, and of looking up and keeping touch with his old schoolfellows and friends.

And then, at last, two or three years before this story opens, and when his uncle was dead, it came to be said about London that Walter Cundall, the richest man from the Pacific to the Gulf of Honduras, had taken a house in Grosvenor Place, and meant to make London more or less permanently his residence. The other places that have been mentioned were purchased one by one, and he used all his possessions—sharing them with his friends—by turn; but London was, as people said, his home. Occasionally he would go off to Honduras on business, or would rush by the Orient express to St. Petersburg or Vienna; but he loved England better than any other spot in the globe, and never left it unless he was obliged to do so.

This was the man whom gossip had said was the future husband of Ida Raughton—this tall, dark, handsome man, who was, when in England, a great deal by her side. But gossip had been rather staggered when it heard that, during Mr. Cundall's last absence of six months in the tropics, she had become the affianced wife of Lord Penlyn! It wondered what he would say when he came back, as it heard he was about to do very shortly, and it wondered why on earth she had taken Penlyn when she might have had Cundall. It talked it over in the drawing-rooms and the ball-rooms, at Epsom and on the lawn at Sandown, but it did not seem to arrive at any conclusion satisfactory to itself.

"I suppose the fact of it is that Cundall never asked her," one said to another, "and she got tired of waiting."

"I should have waited a bit longer on the off chance," the other said "Cundall's a fifty times richer fellow than Penlyn, and there's no comparison between the two. The one is a man of the world and a splendid fellow, and the other is only a boy."

"He isn't a bad sort of a boy though," said a third, "good-looking, and all that. And," he continued sententiously, "he has the pull in age. That's what tells! He is about twenty-five, and Cundall's well over thirty, isn't he?"

"Thirty is no such great age," said the first one, who, being over forty himself, looked upon Cundall also as almost a boy, "and, for my part, I think she has made a mistake!"

And that was what the world said: "She had made a mistake!" Did she think so herself, as she sat there that bright afternoon? No, that could not be possible! Ida Raughton was a girl with too pure and honourable a heart to take one man when she loved another. And we know what the gossips did not know, that no word of love had ever passed between her and Walter Cundall. The world was indulging in profitless speculations when it debated in its mind why Ida had not taken as a husband a man who had never spoken one word of love to her!

CHAPTER II.

A few days after Ida Raughton had been indulging in those summer noontide meditations, Walter Cundall arrived at his house in Grosvenor Place. Things were so well ordered in the establishment of which he was master, that a telegram from Liverpool, despatched a few hours earlier, had been sufficient to cause everything to be in readiness for him; and his servants were so used to his coming and going that his arrival created no unusual excitement.

He walked into his handsome library followed by a staid, grave man-servant, and, sitting down in one of his favourite chairs, said:

"Well, West, what's the news in London?"

"Not much, sir; at least nothing that would interest you. There are a good many balls and parties going on, of course, sir; and next week's Ascot, you know, sir."

"Ascot, is it? Yes, to be sure! We might take a house there, West, and have some friends. The four-in-hand could go over from Cookham—"

"Beg pardon, sir, but I don't think you'll be able to entertain any of your friends this year—not at Ascot, any how. Sir Paul Raughton's man and me were a-talking together, sir, last night at our little place of meeting, and he told me as how Sir Paul was going to have quite a large party down at his place, you know, sir, to celebrate—to celebrate—I mean for Ascot, sir."

"Well?"

"Well, of course, sir, you'll be wanted there too, sir. Indeed, Sir Paul's man said as how his master had been making inquiries about the time you was a-coming back, sir, and said he should like to have you there. And of course they want to cele—I mean to keep it up, sir. Now, I'll go and fetch you the letters that have come since I sent you the last mail."

While the servant was gone, Walter Cundall lay back in his chair and meditated. He was a handsome man, with a dark, shapely head, and fine, well-marked features. He was very brown and sunburnt, as it was natural he should be; but, unlike many whose principal existence has been passed in the Tropics, there was no sign of waste or languor about him. His health during all the years he had spent under a burning Caribbean sun had never suffered; fever and disease had passed him by. Perhaps it was his abstemiousness that had enabled him to escape the deadly effects of a climate that kills four at least out of every ten men. As he sat in his chair he wondered why Providence had been so unfailingly good to him through his life; why it had showered upon him—while he was still young enough to enjoy it—the comforts that other men spent their lives in toiling to obtain, and then often failed at last to get.

"And now," he said to himself, "let Fortune give me but one more gift, and I am content. Let me have as partner of all I possess the fairest woman in the world; let my sweet, gentle Ida tell me that she loves me—as I know she does —and what more can I ask? Ah, Ida!" he went on, apostrophising the woman he loved, "I wonder if you have guessed how, night after night during these long six months, I have sat on my verandah gazing up at the stars that look like moons there, wondering if your dear eyes were looking at them in their feeble glory here? I wonder if you have ever thought during my long absence that not an hour went by, at night or day, when I was not thinking of you? Yes, you must have done so; you must have done so! There was everything in your look, in your voice to tell me that you loved me, that you were only waiting for me to speak. And, now, I will speak. I will deprive myself no longer of the love that will sweeten my life."

The man servant came back with an enormous bundle of letters that made Cundall laugh when he saw them.

"Why, West!" he exclaimed, "you don't imagine that I am going to wade through these now, do you?"

"I think they're mostly invitations, sir," the servant answered, "from people who did not know when you would be back."

"Well, give them to me. I will open a few of those the handwriting of which I recognise, and Mr. Stuart can go through the rest to-morrow."

Mr. Stuart was one of Cundall's secretaries, who, when his employer was in town, had sometimes to work night and day to keep pace with his enormous correspondence, but who was now disporting himself at Brighton. When Cundall was away it was understood that this gentleman should attend four days a week, two at Grosvenor Place, and two at his agent's in the City, but that on others he should be free. As, with his usual generosity, Cundall gave him five hundred a year for doing this, his post was a good one.

The valet came down at this moment to take his master's orders, and to say that his bath was ready.

"I shall dine quietly at the club to-night," Mr. Cundall said, "and then, to-morrow, I will make a few calls, and let my friends know I have returned. Is there anything else, West?"

"No, sir. Oh, I beg pardon, sir! I had almost forgot. Lady Chesterton called the day before yesterday to ask when you would be back. When I told her ladyship you were expected, she left a note for you. It's in that bundle you have selected, I think, sir."

Cundall looked through the letters until he found the one in question, and, on opening it, discovered that it contained an invitation for a ball on that evening. As Lady Chesterton was a hostess whom he liked particularly, he made up his mind that he would look in, if only for an hour. It was as good a way as any of letting people know that he was back in town, and his appearance at her house and at the club would be quite enough to do so.

It was eight o'clock when he entered the latter institution, and his arrival was hailed with a chorus of greeting. A man of colossal wealth is, of course, always welcome amongst his intimates and acquaintances, but, if he is of a reflecting nature, it may be that the idea sometimes occurs to him that he is only appreciated for his possessions, and that, behind his back, there is no such enthusiasm on his behalf as is testified to his face. He does not know, perhaps, of all the sneers and jeers that go on about Cr[oe]sus and Sir Gorgius Midas, but it is to be supposed that he has a very good idea of the manner in which his fellow men regard him. With Walter Cundall it was not thus; men neither scoffed at his wealth nor at him, nor did it ever occur to him to think that he was only liked because of that wealth. There was a charm in his nature, a something in his pleasant words and welcoming smile that would have made him, in any circumstances, acceptable to those with whom he mixed, even though it had not been in his power to confer the greatest benefits upon them. There are many such men as he was, as well as many whom we detest for their moneyed arrogance; men whose lawns and parks and horses and yachts we may enjoy, but with whom, if they could not place them at our disposal, we should still be very happy to take a country walk or spend an hour in a humble parlour.

He was surrounded at once by all kinds of acquaintances, asking questions as to when he had arrived, how he had enjoyed the voyage, what May had been like in the Tropics, what he was going to do in the Ascot week, and a dozen others, some stupid and some intelligent.

"I hardly know about Ascot," he said laughingly, after having answered all the others. "When my old servant, West, reminded me that it was next week, which I had entirely forgotten—by-the-bye, what won the Derby?—I thought of taking a house and having a pleasant lot down, but now I hear that I am wanted at Sir Paul Raughton's."

"Of course you are!" one very young member said, "Rather! Why, you know that—"

"They are going to have a jolly party there," an elder one put in; "no one knows how to manage that sort of thing better than Sir Paul."

Then he turned to the younger man and said, as he drew him aside, "You confounded young idiot! don't you know that he was sweet on Miss Raughton himself, and won't like it when he hears she is engaged to Lord Penlyn? What do you want to make him feel uncomfortable for? He'll hear it quite soon enough."

"I thought he knew it," the other one muttered.

"I imagine not; and I fancy no one but you would want to be the first to tell him."

There was undoubtedly this feeling amongst the group, by whom Cundall was surrounded. Not one of these men, except the boyish member, but was aware that, before he went abroad six months ago, London society was daily expecting to hear that he and the beautiful Ida Raughton were engaged. Now they understood, with that accuracy of perception which men of the world possess in an extraordinary degree, that her recent engagement to Lord Penlyn was unknown to him, and they unanimously determined—though without any agreement between them—that they would not be the first to open his eyes. He was so good a fellow that none of them wanted to cause him any pain; and that the knowledge that Miss Raughton was now engaged would be painful to him, they were convinced.

Two or three of them made up a table and sat down to dinner, and Cundall told them that he was going to Lady Chesterton's later on. But neither here, nor over their coffee afterwards, did any of his friends tell him that he would meet there the girl he was thought to admire, attended in all probability by her future husband, Lord Penlyn.

As, at eleven o'clock, he made his way up the staircase to greet his hostess, he again met many people whom he knew, and, by the time he at last reached Lady Chesterton, it was rapidly being told about the ball-room that Walter Cundall was back in town again.

"I declare you look better than ever," her ladyship said as she welcomed him. "Your bronzed and sunburnt face makes all the other men seem terribly pale and ghastly. How you must enjoy roaming about the world as you do!"

He answered her with a smile and a remark, that, after all, there was no place like London and that he was getting very tired of rambling, when he turned round and saw Ida Raughton coming towards him on the arm of Lord Penlyn.

"How do you do, Miss Raughton?" he said, taking her hand and giving one swift look into her eyes. How beautiful she was, he thought; and as he looked he wondered how he could ever have gone away and left her without speaking of his love. Well, no matter, the parting was over now!

"How are you, Penlyn?" he said, shaking him cordially by the hand.

"When did you return?" Ida asked. Until this moment she had no idea that he was back in England.

"I landed at Liverpool late last night," he answered, "and came up to town to-day. Lady Chesterton, hearing of my probable arrival, was kind enough to leave an invitation for me for to-night."

Before any more could be said the band began to play, and Lord Penlyn turned round to Cundall and said:

"I am engaged for this dance, though it is only a square one. Will you look after Miss Raughton until I return?"

"With pleasure, or until some favoured partner comes to claim her. But," turning to her, "I presume you are also engaged for this dance, 'though it is only a square one.'"

"No," she said, "you know I never dance them."

"Shall we go round the rooms, then?" he asked, offering her his arm. "It is insufferably hot here!"

Lady Chesterton had moved away to welcome some other guests, and so they walked to another part of the room. As Ida looked up at him, she thought how well and strong he seemed, and recalled the many dances they had had together. And she wondered if he was glad to be back in London again?

"How cool and pleasant the conservatory looks!" he said, as they passed the entrance to it. "Shall we go in and sit down until you are claimed for the next dance?"

She assented, and they went in and took possession of two chairs that were standing beneath some great palms and cacti.

"I should think that after the heat you have been accustomed to you would feel nothing in England," she said.

"In Honduras we are suitably clad," he answered, laughing, "and evening dress suits are not in much request. But I am very glad to be wearing one again, and once more talking to you."

"Are you?" she said, raising her eyes and looking at him. She recalled how often they had talked together, and how she had taken pleasure in having him tell her of the different parts of the world he had seen; parts that seemed so strange to her who had never been farther away from home than the Tyrol or Rome.

"Indeed I am! Do you think I should go to the Tropics for pleasure?"

"I suppose you need not go unless you choose," she said; "surely you can do as you please!"

"I can do as I please now," he answered, "I could not hitherto. I will tell you what I mean. Until a month ago the property I owned in Honduras required my constant attention, and necessitated my visiting the place once at least in every two years. But, of late, this has become irksome to me—I will explain why in a moment—and my last visit was made with a view to disposing of that property. This I have made arrangements for doing, and I shall go no more to that part of the world. Now," and his voice became very low, but clear, as he spoke, "shall I tell you why I have broken for ever with Honduras?"

"Yes," she said. "You have told me so often of your affairs that you know I am always interested in them. Tell me."

As she spoke, the band was playing the introduction to the last popular waltz, and the few couples who were in the conservatory left for it. A young man to whom Ida was engaged for this dance came in to look for her, but, seeing that she was talking to Walter Cundall, withdrew. It happened that he did not know she was betrothed to Lord Penlyn, but was aware that, last season, every one thought she would soon be engaged to the man she was now with. So he thought he would not disturb them and went unselfishly away, being seen by neither.

Then, as the strains of the waltz were heard from the ball-room, he said:

"It is because I want to settle down in England and make it my home. Because I want a wife to make that home welcome to me, because I have long loved one woman and have only waited until my return to tell her so. Ida, you are that woman! I love you better than anything in this world! Tell me that you will be my wife!"

For answer she drew herself away from him, pale, and trembling visibly, and trying to speak. But no word came from her lips.

"Why do you not answer me, Ida?" he asked. "Have I spoken too soon? But no! that is not possible—you must have seen how dearly I loved you! how I always sought your presence—you must—"

Then she made a motion to him with her fan, and found her voice.

"You cannot have heard," she said, "no one can have told you that—"

"That what! What is there to tell? For God's sake speak, Ida!"

"That I am engaged."

"Engaged!" he said, rising to his feet. "Engaged! while I have been away. Oh! it cannot be, it is impossible! You must have seen, you must have known of my love for you. It cannot be true!"

"It is true, Mr. Cundall."

"True!" Then he paused a moment and endeavoured to recover himself. When he had done so he said very quietly, but in a deep, hoarse voice: "I congratulate you, Miss Raughton. May I ask who is the fortunate gentleman?"

"I am engaged to Lord Penlyn."

He took a step backward and ejaculated, "Lord Penlyn! Lord—"

Then once more he recovered himself, and said: "Shall I take you back to the ball-room? Doubtless he is looking for you now."

"I am very sorry for your disappointment," she said, looking up at him with a pale face; his emotion had startled her, "very sorry. I would not wound you for the world. And there are so many other women who will make you happy."

"I wanted no other woman but you," he said.

CHAPTER III.

Lord Penlyn and his friend and companion, Philip Smerdon, had returned from their yachting tour, which had embraced amongst other places Le Vocq, about a fortnight before Walter Cundall arrived in London from Honduras. The trip had only been meant to be a short one to try the powers of his new purchase, the *Electra*, but it had been postponed by the storm to some days over the time originally intended. Since he had become engaged to Ida Raughton, he naturally hated to be away from her, and, up till the night before he returned to England, had fretted a great deal at his enforced absence from her.

But the discovery he had made in the *Livre des Étrangers* at Le Vocq, had had such an effect upon his thoughts and mind that, when he returned to England, he almost dreaded a meeting with her. He was an honourable, straightforward man, and, with the exception of being possessed of a somewhat violent and obstinate temper when thwarted in anything he had set his heart upon, had no perceptible failings. Above all he hated secrecy, or secrecy's next-door neighbour, untruth; and it seemed to him that, if not Ida, at least Ida's father, should be told about the discovery he had made.

"With the result," said Philip Smerdon, who was possessed of a cynical nature, "that Miss Raughton would be shocked at hearing of your father's behaviour, and that Sir Paul would laugh at you."

"I really don't see what there is to laugh at in my father being a scoundrel, as he most undoubtedly was."

"A scoundrel!" Philip echoed.

"Was he not? We have what is almost undoubted proof that he was living for two summers at that place with some lady who could not have been his wife, and whom he must have cast off previous to marrying my mother. And there was the child for whom the landlord took me! He must have deserted that as well as the woman. And, if a man is not a scoundrel who treats his offspring as he must have treated that boy, I don't know the meaning of the word."

"As I have said before, it is highly probable that both of them were dead before he married your mother."

"Nonsense! That is a very good way for a novelist to make a man get rid of his encumbrances before settling down to comfortable matrimony, but not very likely to happen in real life. I tell you I am convinced that, somewhere or other, the child, if not the mother, is alive, and it is horrible to me to think that, while I have inherited everything that the Occleves possessed, this elder brother of mine may be earning his living in some poor, if not disgraceful, manner."

"The natural children of noblemen are almost invariably well provided for," Smerdon said quietly; "why should you suppose that your father behaved worse than most of his brethren?"

"Because, if the estate had been charged with anything I should have known it. But it was not—not for a farthing."

"He might have handed over to this lady a large sum down for her and for her son, when they parted."

"Which is also impossible! He was only Gervase Occleve then, and had nothing but a moderately comfortable allowance from his predecessor, his uncle. He married my mother almost directly after he became Lord Penlyn."

This was but one of half-a-dozen conversations that the young men had held together since their return from France, and Gervase had found comfort in talking the affair over and over again with his friend. Philip Smerdon stood in the position to him of old schoolfellow and playmate, of a 'Varsity friend, and, later on, of companion and secretary. Had they been brothers they could scarcely have been—would probably not have been—as close friends as they were.

When they were at Harrow, and afterwards at Christ Church, Oxford, they had been inseparable, and, in point of means, entirely on an equality, Philip's father being a reported, and, apparently, enormously wealthy contractor in the North. But one day, without the least warning, without a word from his father or the slightest stopping of his allowance, he learnt, by a telegram in a paper, that his parent had failed for a stupendous sum, and was undoubtedly ruined for ever. The news turned out to be true, and Philip knew that, henceforth, he would have to earn his own living instead of having a large income to spend.

"Thank God!" he said, in those days, "that I am not quite a fool, and have

21

not altogether wasted my time. There must be plenty of ways in which a Harrow and Oxford man can earn a living, and I mean to try. I have got my degrees, and I suppose I could do something down at the old shop (meaning the old University, and with no disrespect intended), or get pupils, or drift into literature—though they say that means starvation of the body and mortification of the spirit."

"First of all," said Penlyn, who in that time was the counsellor, and not, as he afterwards became, the counselled, "see a bit of the world, and come along with me to the East. When you come back, you will be still better fitted than you are now for doing something or other—and you are young enough to spare a year."

"Still, it seems like wasting time—and, what's worse!—it's sponging on you."

"Sponging! Rubbish! You don't think I am going alone, do you? And if you don't come, somebody else will! And you know, old chap, I'd sooner have you than any one else in the world."

"All right, Jerry," his friend said, "I'll come and look after you."

But when they found themselves in the East, it turned out that the "looking after" had to be done by Penlyn, instead of by Philip. The one was always well, the other always ill. From the time they got to Cairo, it seemed as if every malady that can afflict a man in those districts fell upon Smerdon. At Thebes he had a horrible low fever, from which he temporarily recovered, but at Constantine he was again so ill, that his friend thought he would never bring him away alive. Nor, but for his own exertions, would he ever have done so, and the mountain city would have been his grave. But Gervase watched by his side day and night, was his nurse and doctor too (for the grave Arab physician did nothing but prescribe cooling drinks for him and herbal medicines), bathed him, fanned him, and at last brought him, though weak as a child, back to life.

"How am I ever to repay this?" the sick man said, as he sat up one evening, gazing out on the Algerian mountains and watching the sun sink behind them. "What can I ever do in acknowledgment of your having saved my life?"

"Get thoroughly well, and then we'll go home as fast as we can. And don't talk bosh about repayment."

"Bosh! Do you call it that? Well, I don't suppose I ever shall be able to do anything in return, but I should like to have the chance. As a rule, I don't talk bosh, I believe, though no one is a judge of themselves. Do give me another drink of that lemon-water, Jerry, the thirst is coming on again."

"Which comes of talking nonsense, so shut up!" his friend answered, as he handed him the drink.

"It does seem hard, though, that instead of my being your companion as I came out to be, you should have to always—"

"Now look here, Phil, my friend," Gervase said, "if you *don't* leave off talking, I'll call the doctor." This threat was effectual, for the native physician had such unpleasant personal peculiarities that Philip nearly went mad whenever he entered the room.

Four years have passed since that excursion to the East and the time when Gervase Occleve is the affianced husband of Ida Raughton, but the friendship of these two has only grown more firm. On their return to England, Lord Penlyn offered his friend the post of his secretary combined with steward, which at that moment was vacant by the death of the previous holder. "But companion as well," he said laughingly, "I am not going to have you buried alive at Occleve Chase when I want your society in London, nor *vice versâ*, so you had better find a subordinate."

Smerdon took the post, and no one could say with any truth that his friendship for Lord Penlyn stood in the way of his doing his duty to him as his secretary. He made himself thoroughly master of everything concerning his friend's property—of his tenants and his servants; he knew to a head the cattle belonging to him, and what timber might be marked annually, and regulated not only his country estate but also his town house. And, that his friend should not lose the companionship which he evidently prized so dearly, he thought nothing of travelling half the night from Occleve Chase to London, and of appearing fresh and bright at the breakfast table. For, so deeply had Penlyn's goodness to him in all things sunk into his heart, that he never thought he had done enough to show his gratitude.

Of course in society it was known that, wherever Lord Penlyn went his friend went also, and no doors were shut to the one that were open to the other, or would have been shut had Philip chosen. But he cared little for fashionable doings, and refused to accompany his friend to many of the balls and dinners to which he went.

"Leave me alone in peace to read and smoke," he would say, "and go out and enjoy yourself. I shall be just as happy as you are." And when he learned that Ida Raughton had consented to be Lord Penlyn's wife he told him that he was sincerely glad to hear it. "A man in your position wants a wife," he said, "and you have found a good one in her, I am sure. You will be as happy as I could wish you, and that is saying a good deal."

They had been busy this morning—the morning after Lady Chesterton's ball—in going over their accounts, and in making arrangements for their visit, in the forthcoming Ascot week, to Sir Paul's villa, near the Royal course. Then, while they had paused for a few moments to indulge in a cigarette, the conversation had again turned upon that discovery at Le Vocq.

"I tell you what I do mean to do," Penlyn said, "I mean to go and see Bell. Although he could have known nothing of what was going on thirty years ago, he may have heard his father say something on the subject. They have been our solicitors for years."

"It is only letting another person into the story, as he probably knows nothing about it," Philip said. "I wouldn't go, if I were you."

"I will, though," Penlyn answered; and he did.

Mr. Bell was a solicitor of the modern type that is so vastly different from the old one. Thirty years ago, when our fathers went to consult the family lawyer, they saw either an elderly gentleman with a shaved upper lip and decorous mutton-chop whiskers, or a young man, also with his lip shaved, and clad in a solemn suit of black. But all that is passed, and Mr. Bell was an excellent specimen of the solicitor of to-day. He wore a neatly waxed moustache, had a magnificent gardenia in his well-cut morning coat, and received Lord Penlyn in a handsomely furnished room that might almost have passed for the library of a gentleman of taste. And, had his client been a few years older, they would probably have known each other well at Oxford, for Mr. Bell himself had been a John's man, and had been well known at the debating rooms.

He listened to his client's story, smiling faintly once or twice, at what seemed to his worldly mind, too much remorse for his father's sin on the part of Lord Penlyn, then he said:

"I never even knew your father, but I should think the whole affair a simple one, and an ordinary version of the old story."

"What old story?"

"The story of a person of position— Forgive me, Lord Penlyn, we are men of the world" (he said "we," though he considered his client as the very reverse of "a man of the world"), "and can speak plainly; the story of a person of position taking up with some woman who was his inferior and flattered by his attentions, amusing himself with her till he grew tired, and then— dropping her."

"To starve with her—with his offspring!"

"I should imagine not!" Mr. Bell said with an airy cynicism that made him appear hateful to his young client. "No, I should imagine not! The ladies who attach themselves to men of your father's position generally know how to take very good care of themselves. You may depend that this one was either provided for before she agreed to throw in her lot with him, or afterwards."

The lawyer's opinion was the same as Philip's, and they both seemed to look upon the affair as a much less serious one than it appeared to him! Were they right, and was he making too much out of this peccadillo of his father's?

"And you can tell me nothing further?" he asked the solicitor.

"What can I tell you?" the lawyer said. "I never saw the late Lord Penlyn, and scarcely ever heard my father mention him. If you like I will have all the papers relative to him gone through; but it is thirty years ago! If the lady is alive and had wanted anything, she would surely have turned up by now. And I may say the same of the son."

"He may not even know the claim he has."

"Claim! my lord, what claim? He has no claim on you."

"Has he not? Has he not the claim of brotherhood, the claim that my father deserted his mother? I tell you, Mr. Bell, that if I could find that man I would make him the greatest restitution in my power."

The lawyer looked upon Lord Penlyn, when he heard these words, as a Quixotic young idiot, but of course he did not say so. It occurred to him that, in all probability, his father had had more than one affair of this kind, and he wondered grimly what his romantic young client would say if he heard, by chance, of any more of them. But he did promise to go through all the papers in his possession relating to the late lord, and to see about this particular case. "Though I warn you," he said, "that I am not likely to find anything that can throw any light upon an affair of so long ago. And, as a lawyer, I must say that it is not well that such a dead and gone business should ever be dug up again."

"I would dig it up," Lord Penlyn answered, "for the sake of justice."

Then he went away, leaving the lawyer's mind wavering between contempt and admiration for him.

"He must be a good young fellow at heart, though," Mr. Bell said to himself; "but the world will spoil him."

Two nights afterwards Penlyn received a letter from him, saying that there was not the slightest trace in any of the Occleve papers in his possession of the persons about whom they had spoken. Moreover, Mr. Bell said he had gone through a great many of the accounts of the late Lord Penlyn, and of his uncle and predecessor, but in no case could he find any evidence of the Hon. Gervase having ever exceeded his income, or, when he succeeded to the property, of having drawn any large sum of money for an unknown purpose. "And," he concluded, "I should advise your lordship to banish the whole affair for ever from your mind. If your father really had the intimacy imagined by you with that lady, time has removed all signs of it; and, even though you might be willing to do so, it would be impossible for you now to obtain any information about it."

CHAPTER IV.

Two people went away from Lady Chesterton's ball with anything but happiness at their hearts—Ida Raughton and Walter Cundall. The feelings with which the former had heard the latter's declaration of love had been of a very mixed nature; pity and sympathy for him being combined with an idea that she had not altogether been loyal to the man to whom she was now pledged. She was able to tell herself, as she sat in her dressing-room after her maid had left her, that she had, after all, become engaged to the man whom she really loved; but she had also to acknowledge that, for that other one, her compassion was very great. She had never loved him, nor did she until this night believe the rumours of society that reached her ears, to the effect that he loved her; but she had liked him very much, and his society had always been agreeable to her. His conversation, his stories of a varied life in other lands, had had a charm for her that the invertebrate gossip of an ordinary London salon could never possess; but there her liking for him had stopped. And, for she was always frank even to herself, she acknowledged that he was a man whom she regarded with some kind of awe; a man whose knowledge of the world was as much above hers as his wealth was above her father's wealth. She remembered, that when any question had ever perplexed her, any question of politics, science, or art, to which she could find no answer, he would instantly solve the knotty subject for her, and throw a light upon it that had never come to her mind. Yes, she reflected, he was so much above her that she did not think, in any circumstances, love could have come into her heart for him.

But, if there was no love there was intense sympathy. She could not forget, at least not so soon after the occurrence, his earnest appeal to her to speak, his certainty that she knew of his love, and then the deep misery apparent in his voice when he forced himself into restraint, and could even go so far as to congratulate her. Her knowledge of the world was small, but she thought that from his tone this must have been almost the first, as she was sure it was the greatest, disappointment he had ever had. "He wanted to have a wife to make his home welcome to him," he had said, "and she was the woman whom he wanted for that wife." Surely, she reflected, he was entitled to her pity, though she could not give him her love. And then she wondered what she ought to do with regard to telling her father and her future husband. She did not quite know, but she thought she would tell her father first, and then, if he considered it right that Gervase should know, he should also be told. Perhaps he, too, would feel inclined to pity Mr. Cundall.

As for him, he hardly knew what to do on that night. He walked back to his house in Grosvenor Place (he was too uneasy to sit in his carriage), and, letting himself in went to his library, where he passed some hours pacing up and down it. Once he muttered a quotation from the Old Testament, and once he flung himself into a chair and buried his head in his hands, and wept as strong men only weep in their darkest hour. Afterwards, when he was calmer, he went to a large *écritoire*, and, unlocking it, took out a bundle of papers and read them. They were a collection of several old letters, a tress of hair in an envelope, which he kissed softly, and two slips of paper which he seemed to read particularly carefully. Then he put them away and said to himself: "It must be done, there is no help for it. My happiness is gone for ever, and, God knows, I would not wreck the happiness of others! but, in this case, my sin would be beyond recall if I hesitated." And, again, after a pause, he said to himself: "It must be done."

He rose in the morning at his usual time, though it was nearly six before he flung himself wearily on his bed to snatch some troubled rest, and when he went downstairs to his breakfast he found his secretary, Mr. Stuart, waiting for him. The young fellow had been telegraphed for on his employer's return, and had torn himself away from the charms of Brighton to come back to his duties. After they had exchanged greetings, the secretary said:

"West told me that I should find you looking better than ever, Mr. Cundall, but I cannot honestly say that I do. You look pale and worn."

"I am perfectly well, nevertheless. But I went to a bail last night, and, what with that and travelling all day, I am rather knocked up. But it is nothing. Now, let us get to work on the correspondence, and then we must go into the City."

They began on the different piles of letters, Mr. Cundall throwing over to Stuart all those the handwriting of which he did not recognise, and opening those which he did know himself.

Presently he came to one with a crest on the envelope that he was well acquainted with—the Raughton crest, and he could scarcely resist a start as he saw it. But he controlled himself and tore the letter open. It was from Sir Paul, and simply contained an invitation from him to Cundall to make one of his Ascot party at Belmont, the name of his place near there. The writer said he had heard it rumoured about that he was on his way home from Honduras, and hence the invitation, as if he got back in time, he hoped he would come. This letter had been written some day or two ago, and had been passed over by Cundall on the previous one. Had he not so passed it over, he would have known his fate before he went to Lady Chesterton's ball, for the Baronet went on to say: "You may have learned from some of your numerous correspondents that Ida and Lord Penlyn are engaged. The marriage is fixed for the 1st September, and will, I hope and believe, be a suitable one in every way. At least, I myself can see nothing to prevent its being so; and I shall hope to receive your congratulations, amongst others, when we meet."

He read the letter and put it in his pocket, and then he said to Stuart:

"I have had a letter from Sir Paul Raughton, in which he tells me his daughter is engaged to Lord Penlyn. You go out a good deal, when did you first hear of it?"

The secretary looked up, and seemed rather confused for the moment. He, too, like every one else, even to West the butler, knew that it was supposed that Cundall was in love with Ida, and had wondered what he would say when he heard it. And now he was sitting opposite to him, asking him in the most calm tone when he first knew of her engagement, and the calmness staggered him. Had the world, after all, been mistaken?

"Oh, I don't know," he said. "Not so very long ago. About a month, I should say."

"About a month since it was announced?"

"Yes, about that."

"I wonder you did not think of telling me in your last letter, since you knew how intimate I was with the Raughtons."

"I forgot it. It—it slipped my memory. And there were so many business matters to write about."

"Well! it is of no importance."

"Of no importance!" Stuart thought to himself. "Of no importance!" Then they must all have been indeed mistaken! Why, it was only two or three days before Mr. Cundall's return that he had, when up in town for the day, consulted West, and told him that he had better not say anything on that subject to his master, but let him find it out for himself. And now he sat there calmly reading his letters, and saying that "it was of no importance!" Well, he was glad to hear it! Cundall was a good, upright man, and, when he heard of Ida Raughton's engagement, his first thought had been that it would be a blow to his employer. He was very glad that his fears were ungrounded.

They went to the City together later on, and then they separated; but before they did so, Cundall asked Stuart if he knew what club Lord Penlyn belonged to.

"'Black's,' I fancy, and the 'Voyagers,' but we can see in the Directory." And he turned to the Court department of that useful work, and found that he was right.

In the evening of two days later Cundall called at "Black's," and learned that Lord Penlyn was in that institution.

"Will you tell him, if you please," he said, "that Mr. Cundall wishes to see him?"

All through those two days he had been nerving himself for the interview that was now about to take place, and had at last strung himself up for it. He had prayed that there might be no cruelty in what he was about to do; but he was afraid! The lad—for he was little better—whom he was now summoning, was about to be dealt a blow at his hand that would prostrate him to the earth; he hoped that he would be man enough to bear it well.

"How are you, Cundall?" Lord Penlyn said, coming down the stairs behind the porter, and greeting him with cordiality. "I have never had the pleasure of seeing you here before."

Then he looked at his visitor and saw that he was ghastly pale, and he noticed that his hand was cold and damp.

"Oh, I say!" he exclaimed, "aren't you well? Come upstairs and have something."

"I am well, but I have something very serious to say to you, and—"

"Ida is not ill?" the other asked apprehensively, his first thoughts flying to the woman he loved. And the familiar name upon his lips struck to the other's heart.

"She is well, as far as I know. But it is of her that I have come to speak. This club seems full of members, will you come for a stroll in the Park? It is close at hand."

"Yes, yes!" Penlyn said, calling to the porter for his hat and stick. "But what can you have to say to me about her?"

Then, as they went down St. James' Street and past Marlborough House into the Park, there did come back suddenly to his memory some words he had once overheard about Cundall being in love with the woman who was now his affianced wife. Good God! he thought, suppose he had come to tell him that he held a prior promise from her, that she belonged to him! But no; that was absurd! He had seen her that very day, and, though he remembered that she had been particularly quiet and meditative, she had again acknowledged her love. There could be nothing this man might have to say about her that should be disagreeable for him to hear. Yet, still, the remembrance of that whisper about his love for her disquieted him.

"Now tell me, Mr. Cundall," he said, "what you have to say to me about my future wife."

They had passed through the railings into St. James' Park, and were in one of the walks. The summer sun was setting, and the loiterers and nursemaids were strolling about; but, nevertheless, in this walk it was comparatively quiet.

"I have come to tell you first," Cundall answered, "that, three nights ago, I asked Ida Raughton to be my wife."

"What!" the other exclaimed, "you asked my future—"

"One moment," Cundall said quietly. "I did not know then that she was your future wife. If you will remember, I had only returned to London on that day."

"And you did not know of our engagement?"

"I knew nothing. Let me proceed. In proposing to her and in gaining her love—for she told me that she had consented to be your wife—you have deprived me of the only thing in this world I prize, the only thing I wanted. I came back to England with one fixed idea, the idea that she loved me, and that, when I asked her, she would accept me for her husband."

He paused a moment, and Lord Penlyn said:

"While I cannot regret the cause of your disappointment, seeing what happiness it brings to me, I am still very sorry to see you suffering so."

Cundall took no notice of this remark, though his soft, dark eyes were fixed upon the younger man as he uttered it. Then he continued:

"In ordinary cases when two men love the same woman—for I love her still, Heaven help me and shall always love her; it is my love for her that impels me to say what I am now about to—when two men love the same woman, and one of them gets the acknowledgment of her love, the other stands aside and silently submits to his fate."

Lord Penlyn had been watching him fixedly as the words fell from his lips, and had noticed the calmness, which seemed like the calmness of despair, that accompanied those words. But there was not, however, the calm that accompanies resignation in them, for they implied that, in this case, he did not intend to follow the usual rule.

"You are right in your idea, Mr. Cundall," he answered. "Surely it is not your intention to struggle against what is always accepted as the case?"

"It is not, for since she loves you I must never look upon her face again. But—there is something else?" He paused again for a moment and drew a deep breath, and then he proceeded:

"Are you a strong man?" he asked. "Do you think you can bear a sudden shock?"

"I do not know what you mean, nor what you are driving at!" Lord Penlyn said, beginning to lose his temper at these strange hints and questions. "I am sorry for your disappointment, in one way, but it is not in your power, nor in that of any one else, to come between the love Miss Raughton and I bear to each other."

"Unfortunately it is in my power and I must do it—temporarily, at least. At present, you cannot marry Miss Raughton."

"*What!* Why not, sir? For what reason, pray?"

"Do not excite yourself! Because she and her father imagine that she is engaged to Lord Penlyn, and—"

"What the devil do you mean, sir?" the other interrupted furiously.

"*And,*" Cundall went on, without noticing the interruption, "*you are not Lord Penlyn!*"

"It is a lie!" the other said, springing at him in the dusk that had now set in, "and I will kill you for it." But Cundall caught him in a grasp of iron and pushed him back, as he said hoarsely: "It is the truth, I swear it before Heaven! Your father had another wife who died before he married your mother, and he left a son by her. That man is Lord Penlyn."

Gervase Occleve took a step back and reeled on to a seat in the walk. In a moment there came back to his mind the inn at Le Vocq, the *Livre des Étrangers* there in which he had seen that strange entry, and the landlord's tale. So that woman was his wife and that son a lawful one, instead of the outcast and nameless creature he had pictured him in his mind! But—was this story true?

He rose again and stood before Cundall, and said:

"I do not know how you, who seem to have lived in such out-of-the-way parts of the world, are capable of substantiating this extraordinary statement; but you will have to do so, and that before witnesses. You have brought a charge of the gravest nature against the position I hold. I suppose you are prepared to produce some proof of what you say?"

"I am fully prepared," Cundall said.

"Then I would suggest, Mr. Cundall, that you should call at my house to-morrow, and tell this remarkable tale in full. There will be at least one witness, my friend, Mr. Smerdon. When we have heard what you have to say, we shall know what credence to place in your story."

"I will be there at midday, if you will receive me. And believe me, if it had not been that I could not see Miss Raughton married illegally, and assuming a title to which she had no right, I would have held my peace."

Lord Penlyn had turned away before the last words were spoken, but on hearing them, he turned back again and said:

"Is this secret in your hands only, then, and does it depend upon you alone for the telling? Pray, may I ask who this mysterious Lord Penlyn is whom you have so suddenly sprung upon me?"

"*I am he!*" the other answered.

"You!" with an incredulous stare. "You!"

"Yes, I."

CHAPTER V.

"I have heard it said that he is worth from two to three millions," Philip Smerdon said to his friend the next morning, when Penlyn had, for the sixth or seventh time, repeated the whole of the conversation between him and Cundall. "A man of that wealth would scarcely try to steal another man's title. Yet he must either be mistaken or mad."

"He may be mistaken—I must hope he is—but he is certainly not mad. His calmness last night was something extraordinary, and I am convinced that, provided this story is true, he has told it against his will."

"You mean that he only told it to prevent Miss Raughton from being illegally married, or rather, for the marriage would be perfectly legal since no deception was meant, to prevent her from assuming a title to which she had no claim?"

"Yes."

"You do not think that he hopes by divulging this secret—always assuming it to be true—to cause your marriage to be broken off, so that he might have a chance of obtaining Miss Raughton himself? If his story is true, he can still make her Lady Penlyn."

His friend hesitated. "I do not know," he said. "He bears the character of being one of the most honourable men in London. Supposing his story true, I imagine he was right to tell it."

The young man expressed his opinion and spoke as he thought, but he also spoke in a voice broken with sorrow. If what Cundall had told him was the actual case, not only was he not Lord Penlyn, but he was a beggar. And then Ida Raughton could never be his wife. Even though she might be willing to take him, stripped as he would be of his title and his possessions, it was certain that Sir Paul would not allow her to do so. He began to feel a bitter hatred rising up in his heart against this man, who had only let him enjoy his false position till he happened to cross his path, and had then swooped down upon him, and, in one moment, torn from him everything he possessed in the world. His heart had been full of pity for that unknown and unnamed brother, whom he had imagined to be in existence somewhere in the world; for this man, who was now to come forward armed with all lawful rights to deprive him of what he had so long been allowed blindly to enjoy, he experienced nothing but the blackest hate. For he never doubted for one moment but that the story was true!

At twelve o'clock he and Smerdon were ready to receive the new claimant to all he had imagined his, and at twelve o'clock he arrived. He bowed to Smerdon and held out, with almost a beseeching glance, his hand to Gervase Occleve, but the latter refused to take it.

"Whether your story is true or not," he said, "I have nothing but contempt to give you. If it is false, you are an impostor who shall be punished, socially if not legally; if it is true, you are a bad-hearted man to have left me so long in my ignorance."

"I should have left you so for ever," Cundall answered in a voice that sounded sadly broken, "had it not been for Miss Raughton's sake; I could not see her deceived."

"Had he not come between you and her," Philip. Smerdon asked, "but had wished to marry some other lady, would your scruples still have been the same?"

"No! for she would not have been everything in the world to me, as this one is. And I should never have undeceived him as to the position he stood in. He might have had the title and what it brings with it, I could have given Ida something as good."

"Your ethics are extraordinary!" Philip said, with a sneer.

"You, sir, at least, are not my judge."

"Suppose, sir," Gervase Occleve said, "that you give us the full particulars of your remarkable statement of last night."

"It is hard to do so," Cundall answered. "But it must be done!"

He was seated in a deep chair facing them, they being on a roomy lounge, side by side, and, consequently able to fix their eyes fully upon him. The task he had to go through might have unnerved any man, but he had set himself to do it.

"Before I make any statement," he said, "look at these," and he produced two letters worn with time and with the ink faded. The other took them, and noted that they were addressed to, 'My own dear wife,' and signed, 'Your loving husband, Gervase Occleve.' And one of them was headed 'Le Vocq, Auberge Belle-Vue.'

"Are they in your father's handwriting?" he asked, and Gervase answered "Yes."

"It was in 1852," Cundall said, "that he met my mother. She was staying in Paris with a distant relative of hers, and they were in the habit of constantly meeting. I bear his memory in no respect—he was a cold-hearted, selfish man—and I may say that, although he loved her, he never originally intended to marry her. She told me this herself, in a letter she left behind to be opened by me alone, when I came of age. He won her love, and, as I say, he never intended to marry her. Only, when at last he proposed to her that she should go away with him and be his wife in everything but actual fact, she shrank from him with such horror that he knew he had made a mistake. Then he assumed another method, and told her that he would never have proposed such a thing, but that his uncle, whose heir he was, wished him to make a brilliant match. However, he said he was willing to forego this, and, in the eyes of the world at least, to remain single. For her sake he was willing to forego it, if she also was willing to make some sacrifice. She asked what sacrifice he meant, and, he said the sacrifice of a private marriage, of living entirely out of the world, of never being presented to any of his friends. Poor creature! She loved him well at that time—is it necessary for me to say what her answer was?"

He paused a moment, and he saw that the eyes of Gervase were fixed upon him, but he saw no sympathy for his dead mother in them. Perhaps he did not expect to see any!

"How she explained matters to the relation she lived with, I do not know," he went on; "but they were married in that year in London."

"At what church?" Gervase asked.

"At 'St. Jude's, Marylebone.' Here is the certificate." Gervase took it, glanced at it, and returned it to him.

"Go on," he said, and his voice too had changed.

"They lived a wandering kind of life, but, in those days, a not altogether unhappy one. But at last he wearied of it—wearied of living in continental towns to which no one of their own country ever came, or in gay ones where they passed under an assumed name, that which had been her maiden name—Cundall. At my birth he became more genial for a year or so, and then again he relapsed into his moody and morose state—a state that had become almost natural to him. He began to see that the secret could not be kept for ever, now that he had a son; that some day, if I lived, I must become Lord Penlyn. And he did not disguise his forebodings from her, nor attempt to throw off his gloom. She bore with him patiently for a long while—bore his repinings and taunts; but at last she told him that, after all, there was no such great necessity for secrecy, that she was a lady by birth, a wife of whom he need not be ashamed. Then—then he cursed her; and on the next occasion of their dispute he told her that they had better live apart.

"She took him at his word, and when he woke the next morning she was gone, taking me with her. He never saw her nor me again, and when he heard that she was dead he believed that I was dead also."

"Then he was the deceived and not the deceiver!" Gervase exclaimed. "He thought that I was really his son and heir."

"Yes, he thought so. My mother's only other relative in the world was her brother, a merchant in Honduras, who was fast amassing a stupendous fortune —the one I now possess. She wrote to him telling him that she had married, that her husband had treated her badly, and that she had left him and resumed her maiden name. *His* name she never would reveal. My uncle wrote to say that in such circumstances, and being an unmarried man, he would adopt me as his own child, and that I should eventually be his heir. Then he sent money over for my schooling and bringing up."

He paused again, and again he went on; and it seemed as if he was mustering himself for a final effort.

"When I was little over four years old she died. On her death-bed her heart relented, and she thought that she would do for him what appeared to be the greatest service in her power. She wrote to tell him she was dying, and that he would, in a few days, receive confirmation of her death from a sure hand. *And she told him that I had died two months before.* Poor thing! she meant well, but she was a simple, unworldly woman, and she had no idea of what she was doing. Perhaps it never occurred to her that he would marry again; perhaps she even thought that her leaving him would free him and his from all obligations to me. At any rate, she died in ignorance of the harm she had done, and I am glad she never realised her error."

He paused; and Gervase said:

"Is that all?"

"With the exception of this. When I was twenty-one this letter of my mother's, which no other eyes but mine have ever seen before, was put into my hand. I was then in Honduras, and it had been left in my uncle's care. At first the news staggered me, and I could not believe it. I had always thought my uncle was on my father's side, and not on my mother's, and I now questioned him on the subject. I found that he, himself, was only partly in her secret, and that he knew nothing of my father's real position. Then, as to the names of Occleve and Penlyn, I was ignorant of them; although I had at that age seen something of European society. I came to England shortly afterwards, and there was in my mind some idea of putting in a claim to my birthright. But, on my arrival, I found that another—you—had taken possession of it. You were pointed out to me one night at a ball; and, as I saw you young and happy, and heard you well-spoken of, I put away from me, for ever, all thoughts of ever taking away from you what you—through no fault of your own—had wrongfully become possessed of."

"Yet now you will do so, because I have gained Ida's love."

"No, no, no!" he answered. Then he said, with a sadness that should have gone to their hearts: "I have been Esau to your Jacob all my life. It is natural you should supplant me now in a woman's love."

"What then do you mean to do, *Lord Penlyn?*" Gervase asked bitterly. The other started, and said:

"Never call me by that name again. I have given it to you."

"Perhaps," Smerdon said, with a bitter sneer, "because you are not quite sure yet of your own right to it. You would have to prove that there was a male child of this marriage, and then that you were he. That would not be so easy, I imagine."

"There is nothing would be more easy. I have every proof of my birth and my identity."

"And you intend to use them to break off my marriage with Ida Raughton," Gervase Occleve said.

"For God's sake do not misunderstand me!" Cundall answered. "I simply want you to tell her and her father all this, and be married as Gervase Occleve. I cannot be her husband—I have told you I shall never see her face again—all I wish is that she shall be under no delusion. As for the title, that would have no charms for me, and you cannot suppose that I, who have been given so much, should want to take your property away from you."

"You would have me live a beggar on your charity!—and that a charity which you may see fit to withdraw at any moment, as you have seen fit to suddenly disclose yourself at the most important crisis of my life." He spoke bitterly, almost brutally to the other, but he could rouse him to no anger. The elder brother simply said:

"God forgive you for your thoughts of me!"

"And now," Gervase said, "perhaps you will tell me what you wish done. I shall of course inform Sir Paul Raughton that, in my altered circumstances, my marriage with his daughter must be abandoned."

"No, no!"

"Yes! I say. It will not take twenty-four hours to prove whether you are right in your claim, for if I see the certificate of your birth it will be enough—"

"It is here," Cundall said, producing it. "You can keep it, or take a copy of it."

"Very well. That, and the marriage proved, I will formally resign everything to you, even the hand of Miss Raughton. That is what you mean to obtain by this declaration, in spite of your philanthropical utterances."

"It is false!" Cundall said, roused at last to defend himself, "and you know it. She loves you. You do not imagine I should want to marry her since I have learnt that."

"I do imagine it, for had you been possessed of the sentiments you express, you would have held your tongue. Had you kept silence, no harm could have been done!"

"The worst possible harm would have been done."

"No one on earth but you knew this story until yesterday, and it was in your power to have let it remain in oblivion. But, though you have chosen to bring it forward, there is one consolation still left to me. In spite of your stepping into my shoes, in spite of your wealth—got Heaven knows how!— you will never have Ida Raughton's love. No trick can ever deprive me of that, though she may never be my wife."

"Your utterances of this morning at least prove you to be unworthy of it," Cundall answered, stung at last to anger. "You have insulted me grossly, not only in your sneers about my wealth and the manner it has been obtained, but also by your behaviour. And I have lost all compassion for you! I had intended to let you tell this story in your own way to Sir Paul Raughton and his daughter, but I have now changed my mind. When they return to town, after Ascot next week, I shall call upon Sir Paul and tell him everything. Even though you, yourself, shall have spoken first."

"So be it! I want nothing from you, not even your compassion. To-night I shall leave this house, so that I shall not even be indebted to you for a roof."

"I am sorry you have taken it in this light," Cundall said, again calming himself as he went to the door. "I would have given you the love of a brother had you willed it."

"If you give me the feeling that I have for you, it is one of utter hatred and contempt! Even though you be my brother, I will never recognise you in this world, either by word or action, as anything but my bitterest foe!"

Cundall looked fixedly at him for one moment, then he opened the door and went out.

Philip Smerdon had watched his friend carefully through the interview, and, although there was cause for his excitement, he was surprised at the transformation that had taken place in him. He had always been gentle and kind to every one with whom he was brought into contact; now he seemed to have become a fury. Even the loss of name, and lands, and love seemed hardly sufficient to have brought about this violence of rage.

"It would almost have been better to have remained on friendly terms with him, I think," he said. "Perhaps he thought he was only doing his duty in disclosing himself."

"Perhaps so!" the other said. "But, as for being friendly with him, damn him! I wish he were dead!"

CHAPTER VI.

Sir Paul Raughton's Ascot party had been excellently arranged, every guest being specially chosen with a view to making an harmonious whole. Belmont was a charming villa, lying almost on the borders of the two lovely counties of Berkshire and Surrey, and neither the beauties of Nature nor Art were wanting. Surrounded by woods in which other villas nestled, it was shut off from the world, whilst its own spacious lawns and gardens enclosed it entirely from the notice of passers-by. It was by no means used only during Ascot week, as both Ida and her father were in the habit of frequently paying visits to it in the spring, summer, and autumn; and only in the winter, when the trees were bare, and the wind swept over the heath and downs, was it deserted.

On this Ascot week, or to be particular, this Monday of Ascot week, when the guests were beginning to arrive for the campaign, it was as bright and pretty a spot as any in England. The lawn was dotted with two or three little umbrella tents, under which those arrivals, who were not basking under the shadow of trees, were seated; some of them talking of what they had done since last they met; some engaged in speculating over the chances of the various horses entered for the "Cup," the "Stakes," and the "Vase;" some engaged in idly sipping their afternoon tea (or their afternoon sherry and bitters, as the sex might be), and some engaged in the most luxurious of all pursuits—doing nothing. Yet, although Sir Paul's selection of guests had been admirable, disappointment had come to him and Ida, for two who would have been the most welcome, Mr. Cundall and Lord Penlyn, had written to say they could not come. The former's letter had been very short, and the explanation given for his refusal was that he was again preparing to leave England, perhaps for a very long period. And Lord Penlyn's had been to the effect that some business affairs connected with his property would prevent him from leaving town during the week. Moreover, it was dated from a fashionable hotel in the West End, and not from Occleve House.

"What the deuce can the boy be doing?" the Baronet asked himself, as he read the letter over once or twice before showing it to his daughter. They were seated at breakfast when it came, and none of the guests having arrived, they were entirely by themselves. "What the deuce can he be doing?" he repeated. "Ascot week of most weeks in the year, is the one in which a man likes to get out of town, yet instead of coming here he goes and stews himself up in a beastly hotel! And Cundall, too! Why can't the man stop at home like a Christian, instead of going and grilling in the Tropics? He can't want to make any more money, surely!" After which reflections he handed both the letters over to Ida. When she read them she was sorely troubled, for she could not help imagining that there was something more than strange in the fact that the man who was engaged to her, and the man who had proposed to her only a few nights ago, should both have abstained from coming to spend the week with them. At first, she wondered if they could have met and quarrelled—but then she reflected that that was not possible! Surely Mr. Cundall would not have told Gervase that he had proposed to her and been refused. Men, she thought, did not talk about their love affairs to one another; certainly the rejected one would not confide in the accepted. Still, she was very troubled! Troubled because the man she loved, and whom she had not seen for three days—and it seemed an eternity!—would not be there to pass that happy week with her; and troubled also because the man whom she did not love, but whom she liked and pitied so, was evidently sore at heart. "He was going away again, perhaps for a very long period," he had said, yet, on the night of Lady Chesterton's ball, he had told her that he would go no more away. It must be, she knew, that her rejection of him was once more driving him to be a wanderer on the earth, and, womanlike, she could not but feel sorry for him. She knew as well as Rosalind that men, though they died, did not die for love; but still they must suffer for their unrequited love. That he would suffer, the look in his face and the tone of his voice on that night showed very plainly; his letter to her father and his forthcoming departure told her that the suffering had begun.

Fortunately for her the arrivals of the guests, and her duties as hostess, prevented her from having much time for reflection. The visitors had come to be amused, and she could not be *distraite* or forgetful of their comfort. The gentlemen might look after themselves and amuse each other, as they could do very well with their sporting newspapers and Ruff's Guides, their betting-books and their cigars; but the ladies could not be neglected. So, all through that long summer day, Ida, whose mind was filled with the picture of two men, had to put her own thoughts out of sight, and devote herself to the thoughts of others. She had to listen to the rhapsodies of a young lady over her presentation at Court, to how our gracious Queen had smiled kindly on her, and to how the world seemed full of happiness and joy; she had to listen to the bemoanings of an elderly lady as to the manner in which her servants behaved, and to sympathise with another upon the way in which her son was ruining himself with baccarat and racing. And she had to enter into full particulars as to all things concerning her forthcoming marriage, to give exact accounts of the way in which M. Delaruche was preparing her *trousseau*, and of what alterations were to be made in Occleve House in London, and at Occleve Chase in the country, for her reception; to hear the married ladies congratulate her on the match she was making, and the younger ones gush over the manly perfections of her future husband. But she had also to tell them all that he would not be there this week, and to listen to the chorus of astonishment that this statement produced..

"Not here, my dear Ida," the elderly lady, whose servants caused her so much trouble, said. "Not here. Why, what a strange future husband! To leave you alone for a whole week, and such a week, too, as the Ascot one." And the elderly lady—whose husband at that moment was offering to take four to one in hundreds from Sir Paul that Flip Flap won his race—shook her head disapprovingly.

"Nothing will induce my son to stay away from Ascot," the mother of the gambling young man said to herself. "He will be here to-night, though he is not engaged to Ida." And the poor lady sighed deeply.

"I did so want to see him," the young lady who had just been presented, remarked. "You know I have never met Lord Penlyn yet, and I am dying to know him. They say he is *so* good-looking."

Ida answered them all as well as she could, but she found it hard to do so. And before she had had more than time to make a few confused remarks on his being obliged to stop away, on account of business connected with his property, another unpleasantness occurred.

"I have just heard very bad news, Miss Raughton," a tall gentleman remarked, who had joined the group of ladies. "Sir Paul tells me that Cundall isn't coming for the week. I'm particularly upset, for I wanted him to give me some introductions in Vienna, to which I am just off, you know."

Again the chorus rose, and again poor Ida had to explain that Mr. Cundall was preparing to go abroad once more for a long period. And, as she made the explanation, she could not keep down a tell-tale blush. Seated in that group was more than one who had once thought that, if she loved any man, that man was Walter Cundall.

"He doesn't care for horse-racing, I imagine," the ill-used mother said.

"No more should I," the tall gentleman remarked, "if I had his money. What fun could a race be to him, when a turf gamble would be like a drop in the ocean to a man of his tremendous means?"

"And I have never seen *him* either," the *débutante* remarked, with a look that was comically piteous. "Oh, dear! this is something dreadful! Just think of both Lord Penlyn and Mr. Cundall being absent."

"Don't you think some of us others can supply their places?" the gentleman asked. "We will try very hard, you know!"

"Oh, yes! of course," she replied; "but then we know you, and we don't—at least, I don't—know them. And then you care about racing, and will be thinking of nothing but the horrid horses."

"I will promise to think about nothing but you," he said, lowering his voice, "if you will let me."

At dinner, things were more comfortable for Ida. All the visitors knew now that Penlyn and Cundall were certain absentees, and, having once discussed this, they found plenty of other things to talk about. Sir Paul had got all his guests well assorted, even to the melancholy mother, who took comfort from the words of wisdom that dropped from the mouth of the gentleman who wanted to back Flip Flap: "Let the boy have his fling, madam, let him have his fling! There is nothing sickens a man so much of gambling as an unlimited opportunity of indulging in it. Give him this, and then, if he loses, pull him up sharp on his allowance, and he'll be all right. When he finds he has no more money to squander, he will either play so carefully that he will begin to win, or he'll throw it up altogether. That is what they generally do." It seemed, however, from his conversation, that he had never done that himself.

Miss Norris, the young lady in her first season, was gradually getting over, or, indeed, had got over, her disappointment, and now seemed very comfortable with Mr. Fulke, the tall gentleman. He was a man of the world as well as of society, and knew everybody, and she began to think that, after all, she could support the absence of Lord Penlyn and Mr. Cundall.

So the first night passed away very pleasantly, and Sir Paul congratulated himself on the prospect of a pleasant week. Of course, as was natural, a gentleman would occasionally interrupt a conversation with his neighbour; a conversation on balls and dinners, and the opera, and the last theatrical production; by leaning across the table and saying to another gentleman, "I'll take you five to four in tenners, or ponies, about that;" or, "you can have three hundred to one hundred it doesn't win, if you like;" and, of course, also, there would be the production of little silver-bound books afterwards, and some hasty writing. But on the whole, though, the introduction of the state of Lady Matilda's legs into the conversation, until it turned out that she was a mare who was first favourite for the Cup, did rather dismay some of the fairer portion of the guests, everything was very nice and comfortable.

It was a hot night, an overpoweringly hot night, and every one was glad to escape from the dining-room on to the lawn, where the footmen had brought out lamp-lit tables for the coffee. It seemed to the guests that there must be a thunderstorm brewing; indeed, towards London, where there were heavy banks of lurid clouds massed together, flashes of lightning were occasionally seen, and the thunder heard rolling. But the gentlemen even derived consolation from this, and said that a good storm would make the course— which was as hard as a brick floor—better going, and would lay the dust on the country roads.

At eleven o'clock the last guest, Mr. Montagu, the sportive son of the sad lady, arrived, and, as he brought the latest racing information from town, was eagerly welcomed.

"Yes," he said, after he had kissed his mother and had told her she needn't bother herself about him, he was all right enough. "Yes! the favourites are steady. I dropped into the 'Victoria' before coming over to Waterloo, and took a look at the betting. There you are! And here's the 'Special.'"

These were eagerly seized on and perused. Lady Matilda's legs, which had been the cause of anxiety in the racing world for the past week, seemed to be well enough to give her followers confidence; Mon Roi, another great horse, was advancing in the betting; Flip Flap was all right, and Sir Paul felt thankful he had not laid that bet of four hundred to one hundred in the afternoon; and The Landlord was being driven back. It took another hour for the gentlemen to get all their opinions expressed, and then they went to their rooms, the ladies having long since retired.

"Don't oversleep yourselves, any of you!" Sir Paul Raughton called out cheerily. "We ought to get the four-in-hands under weigh by half-past eleven at latest. Breakfast will be ready as soon as the earliest of you."

Ida went to her room tired with the day's exertions; but her night's rest was very broken. In the early part, the flashing of the lightning and the roar of the thunder (the storm having now broken over the neighbourhood) kept her awake, and when she slept she did so uneasily, waking often. Once she started up and listened tremblingly, as though hearing some unaccustomed sound, and even rose and opened her door, and looked into the passage. "Of what was she afraid?" she asked herself. The house was full of visitors; it was, of all times, the least one likely for harm to come. Then she went back to bed and eventually slept again, though only to dream. Her brain must have retained what she had read in Walter Cundall's letter that morning, for she dreamt that he was taking his farewell of her; only it seemed that they were back again in the conservatory attached to Lady Chesterton's ball-room. She was seated in the same place as she had been when he told her of his love; she could hear the dreamy strains of the very same waltz—nothing was changed, except that it seemed darker, much darker; and she could do little more than recognise his form and see his dark, sad eyes fixed on her. Then he bent over her and kissed her gently on the forehead—more, as it seemed in her dream, with a brother's than a lover's kiss—and said: "Farewell, for ever! In this world we two shall never meet again." Then, as he turned to go, she saw behind him another form with its face shrouded, but with a figure that seemed wonderfully familiar to her, and, as he faced it, it sprang upon him. And with a shriek she awoke—awoke to see the bright sun shining in through her windows, to hear the birds singing outside, and to notice that the hands of the clock pointed to nearly eight.

And her first action was to kneel by the side of her bed and to thank God that it was only a dream.

CHAPTER VII.

There were no late risers at Belmont on that morning, for even the elder ladies, who were not going to Ascot but meant to remain at home and pass the day pleasantly in their own society, made it a point of being early. The younger ones, with Miss Norris the very first down, were a sight that was charming to the gentlemen, with their pretty new gowns prepared especially for the occasion; but of them all, none looked fairer than Ida. Her disturbed rest had made her, perhaps, a little paler than usual, but had thus only added a more delicate tinge to her loveliness. As she stood talking to young Montagu on the verandah, this youth began to wish that he was Lord Penlyn, and to think that there were other things in the world better than going *Banco* or backing winners—or losers! Indefatigable in everything connected with sport, the young man, in company with two other visitors, officers who had been in India and had become accustomed to early rising, had already ridden over to Ascot to learn what was going on there, and to see if any information could be picked up.

"And now, Miss Raughton," he said, "to breakfast with what appetite we can? And I can assure you that, if old Wolsey had only half as good a one as mine is now, King Hal wouldn't have frightened him into saying, 'good-bye' to all the good things in life."

Ida laughed at his nonsense, and then, every one being down, the first important part of the day's proceedings began.

The story of an Ascot party has been told so often and so well, that no other pen is needed to describe it. There are few of us who, either in long vanished or in very recent days, have not formed part in one of these pleasant outings; who have not sat upon a coach, with some young lady beside us, who seemed, at least for the time being, to be the prettiest and nicest girl in the world; who have not eaten our fill of lobster salad and pigeon pie, and drunk our fill of champagne and claret cup!

Sir Paul's party went through it all; the gentlemen (with Mr. Montagu very busy at this) dashing across the course between each race, and into the Grand Stand to "see about the odds." Flip Flap disgraced himself terribly in the Gold

Vase, and came in last of all, much to Sir Paul's disgust, who regretted now that he had not laid his old friend four to one in hundreds, but to the intense delight of young Montagu, who had persuaded Fulke to take the same odds in tens from him.

"Hoorah!" he cried, as the beaten favourite came in with the crowd, "now, if 'Tilda will only pull off the Stakes, I am bound to score heavily to-day."

And he dashed off across the course again, to see what the betting was about the magnificent mare whose name he so familiarly shortened.

Ida sat very peacefully on the coach listening to all the laughter and conversation that was going on around her, but taking very little part in it, except when directly spoken to. But in the intervals, when it was not necessary for her to join in it, her mind reverted to things and persons far away from the bright, sunny racecourse. In her heart, she did feel hurt that, whatever important business transactions he might have, her lover could not find time to run down for even one day. It was evidently supposed by some one that he was with her, for only that morning a letter had come to Belmont for him, a letter which she had instantly reposted to the hotel he was staying at accompanied by a loving one from herself which she had found time to write hastily. It had seemed to her that she knew the handwriting, and she supposed it must be from some common friend of theirs; but, whoever the writer was, he evidently thought Gervase was with them. She supposed he really was very much occupied, but still she wished he would come for one day; and she made up her mind to write to him again that night, and ask him to run down for the Cup. He could leave town at midday and be back at seven; surely he could spare that much time to her! Nor had she forgotten her dream, her horrid dream, and she wondered over and over again why she should have had such a dreadful one, and why last night? Perhaps it was the storm that had affected her!

Once more young Montagu's star was in the ascendant, for Lady Matilda beat all her adversaries, and, to use a sporting phrase, "romped in" for the Stakes. There was great rejoicing over this on the Belmont coaches, of which there were two, one driven by Sir Paul and one by Mr. Fulke; for most of them had backed her with the bookmakers, and so, while they all won, there was no loser in the party. Miss Norris, too, had won a dozen of gloves from Fulke, who took the field against the horse he fancied to oblige the girl he admired, and Sir Paul had promised Ida anything she liked to ask for if Lady Matilda only got home first.

Of course, after the last race, there was an adjournment of the whole party to the lawn; who goes to Ascot without also going to sit for a while in one of the prettiest scenes attached to a racecourse in England? There, seated on comfortable chairs on that soft velvet lawn, with the hot June sun sinking conveniently behind the Grand Stand, the party remained peacefully and chatted until the horses should be put to.

It was at this time that, to the different groups scattered about, there came a rumour that a horrible murder had been committed in London last night, or early that morning. A few persons, who had come down by the last special train, had heard something about it, but they did not know anything of the details; and two or three copies of the first editions of the evening papers had arrived, but they told very little, except that undoubtedly a murder had taken place, and that the victim was, to all appearances, a gentleman. Had it been a common murder in the Seven Dials, or the East End, it would hardly have aroused attention at aristocratic Ascot.

Young Montagu first heard it from a bookmaker with whom he was having a satisfactory settlement, but that worthy knew nothing except that "some one said it was a swell, and that he had been stabbed to the 'eart in the Park."

"Get a paper, Montagu," the baronet said, "and let us, see what it is. Every one seems to be discussing it."

"Easier said than done, Sir Paul!" the other answered. "But I'll try."

He came back in a few moments, having succeeded in borrowing a second edition from a friend, and he read out to them the particulars, which were by no means full. It appeared that, after the storm in London was over, which was about three o'clock in the morning, a policeman going on his walk down the Mall of St. James' Park, had come across a gentleman lying by the railings that divide that part of it from the gardens, a gentleman whom he at first took to be overcome by drink. On shaking him, however, he discovered him to be dead, and he then thought that he must have been struck by lightning. A further glance showed that this was not the case, as he perceived that the dead man was stabbed in the region of the heart, that his watch and chain had been wrenched away (there being a broken piece of the chain left in the button-hole), and, if he had any, his papers and pocket-book taken. His umbrella, which was without any name or engraving, was by his side his linen, which was extremely fine, was unmarked, and his clothes, although drenched with mud and rain, were of the best possible quality. That, up to now, was all the information the paper possessed.

"How dreadful to think of a man being murdered in such a public place as that!" Ida said. "Surely the murderer cannot long escape!"

"I don't know about that," Mr. Fulke said. "The Mall at three o'clock in the morning, especially on such a morning—what a storm it was!—is not very much frequented. A man walking down it might easily be attacked and robbed!"

"It is a nice state of affairs, when a gentleman cannot walk about London without being murdered," Sir Paul said. "But horrible things seem to happen every day now."

The public were leaving the lawn by this time, and one of the grooms came over to say that the coaches were ready. There was no longer anything to stay for, and so they all went back and took their places, and started for Belmont.

It was a glorious evening after a glorious day; and as they went along, some laughing and talking, some flirting, and some discussing the day's racing and speculating on that of the morrow, they had forgotten all about the tragedy they had heard of half-an-hour earlier. Not one of them supposed that the murdered man was likely to be known to them, nor that that crime had broken up their Ascot week. But when they had returned to Belmont, and gone to their rooms to dress for dinner, they learnt that the dead man was known to most of them. A telegram had come to Sir Paul from his butler in London, saying: "The gentleman murdered in St. James' Park last night was Mr. Cundall. He has been identified by his butler and servants."

CHAPTER VIII.

About the same time that Sir Paul Raughton received the telegram from London, and was taking counsel with one or two of his elder guests as to whether he should at once tell Ida the dreadful news or leave it till the morning, Lord Penlyn entered his hotel in town. A change had come over the young man—a change of such a nature that any one, who had seen him twenty-four hours before, would scarcely have believed him to be the same person. His face, which usually bore a good colour, was ghastly pale, his eyes had great hollows and deep rings round them, and even his lips looked as if the blood had left them. He had come from his club—where, since it had been discovered who the victim of last night's tragedy was, nothing else but the murder had been talked about, as was also the case in every club and public place in London—and he now mounted the steps of the hotel with the manner of a man who was either very weak or very weary.

"Do you know where my servant is?" he asked of the hall porter, who held the door open for him; and even this man noticed that his voice sounded strange and broken, and that he looked ill.

"He is at his tea, my lord; shall I send for him?"

"No, but send him to me when he has finished. We shall return to my house to-night."

The porter bowed, and said, "I have sent a letter to your room, my lord," and Penlyn went on. His apartment, consisting of a sitting-room and bed-room, was on the ground floor of the hotel, and was usually given to guests of distinction (who were likely, in the landlord's opinion, to pay handsomely for the accommodation), as it saved them the trouble of going up any stairs. The hotel was a private one; a house that did not welcome persons of whom it knew nothing, but made those whom it did know, entirely at their ease. It was very quiet, shutting its doors at midnight unless any of its visitors were at a ball or party, in which case, if some of those visitors were ladies, the porter's deputy sat up for them; but, when they were gentlemen, furnishing them with latch-keys. As sometimes there were not more than three or four gentlemen in this extremely select hotel at one time, this was an obviously better system than having a night-porter.

Lord Penlyn took up the letter that was lying on his table, and proceeded to open it, throwing himself at the same time wearily into an arm-chair. He recognised Ida's handwriting, and as he did so he wondered if, by any possibility, the letter could be about the subject of which all London was talking to-day–the murder of Walter Cundall. When he saw that there was another one inclosed in it, the handwriting of which he did not know, his curiosity was so aroused (for he wondered how a stranger to him should know, or suppose, that he was at Belmont), that he opened this one first and read it. Read it carefully from beginning to end, and then dropped it on the floor as he put his hands up to his head, and wailed, "Murdered! Oh my God! Murdered! When he had written this letter only an hour before." And then he wept long and bitterly.

The letter ran:

My Brother,

"Since I saw you last Saturday I have been thinking deeply upon what passed between us, and I have come to the conclusion that, after all, it will be best for nothing to be said to any one on the subject of our father's first marriage; not even to Miss Raughton or her father. By keeping back the fact that you have an elder brother, no harm is done to any one. I shall never marry

49

now, and consequently, you are only taking possession of what will be yours, or your children's, eventually. No one but you, your friend Mr. Smerdon, and I, know of this secret; let no one ever know it. We love the same woman, and, when she is your wife, I shall have the right to love her with a brother's love. Let us unite together to make her life as perfectly happy as possible. To do this we must not begin by undeceiving her as to the position she is to hold.

"I suggest this, nay, I command you to do this, because of my love for her, a love which desires that her life may be without pain or sorrow. I shall not witness her happiness with you, not yet at least, for I do not think I could bear that; but, in some future years, it may be that time will have so tempered my sorrow to me, that I shall be able to see you all in all to each other, perhaps to even witness your children playing at her knee, and to feel content. I pray God that it may be so.

"Remember, therefore, what I, by my right as your elder brother—which I exert for the first and last time!—charge you to do. Retain your position, still be to the world what you have been, and devote your life to her.

"I have one other word to say. The Occleve property is a comfortable, though not a remarkably fine, one. You have heard of my means, and they are scarcely exaggerated. If, at any time, there is any sum of money you or she may want, come to me and you shall have it.

"Let us forget the bitter words we each spoke in our interview. Our lives are bound up in one cause, and that, and our relationship, should prevent their ever being remembered.

"Your brother,

"WALTER."

When he was calmer, he picked the letter up again and read it through once more, having carefully locked his door before he did so, for he did not wish his valet to see his emotion. But the re-reading of it brought him no peace, indeed seemed only to increase his anguish. When the man-servant knocked at his door he bade him go away for a time, as he was engaged and could not be disturbed; and then he passed an hour pacing up and down the room, muttering to himself, starting at the slightest sound, and nearly mad with his thoughts. These thoughts he could not collect; he did not know what steps to take next. What was he to tell Ida or Sir Paul—or was he to tell them anything? The dead man, the murdered brother, had enjoined on him, in what he could not have known was to be a dying request, that he was to keep the secret. Why then should he say anything? There was no need to do so! He was Lord Penlyn now, there was nothing to tell! No one but Philip, who was trustworthy, knew that he had ever been anything else. No one would ever know it. And he shuddered as he thought that, if the world did ever know that Walter Cundall had been his brother, then the world would believe him to be his murderer! No! it must never be known that he and that other were of the same blood.

He could not sit still, he must move about, he must leave the house! He rang for his man and told him to pack up and pay the bill, and take his things round to Occleve House, and that he should arrive there late; and the man seemed surprised at his orders.

"Will you not dress, my lord?" he asked. "You were to dine out to-night."

"To-night? Yes! true! I had forgotten it; but I shall not go. Mr. Cundall who was killed last night was a friend of mine; I am going to his club to hear if any more particulars have been made known." And then he went out.

The valet was a quiet, discreet man, but as he packed his master's portmanteaus he reflected a good deal on the occurrences of the past few days. First of all, he remembered the visit of Mr. Cundall on Saturday to Occleve House, and that the footman had told him that he had heard some excited conversation going on as he had passed the room, though he had not been able to catch the words and he also called to mind that, an hour afterwards, Lord Penlyn had told him to take some things round to this hotel (which they were now leaving as suddenly as they had come), and also that they would not pay their visit to Sir Paul Raughton's for the Ascot week. Was there any connecting link between Mr. Cundall's visit to his master, and his master leaving the house and giving up Ascot? And was there any connection between all this and the murder of Mr. Cundall, and the visible agitation of Lord Penlyn? He could not believe it, but still it did seem strange that this visit of Mr. Cundall's should have been followed by such an alteration of his master's plans, and by his own horrible death.

"What time did my governor come in last night?" he said to the porter, as he and that worthy stood in the hall waiting for a cab that had been sent for.

"I don't know," the porter answered. "There was only his lordship and another gent staying in the house, except the Dean's family upstairs, and some foreign swells, and none of them keep late hours, so we gave him and the other gent a key and left a jet of gas burning in the 'all. But both on 'em must have come in precious late, for Jim, who sleeps on the first floor, said he never heard either of them. I say, this is a hawful thing about this Mr. Cundall."

51

"It is so! Well, there's the cab. Jim, put the portmanteaus on the top. Here you are, porter!" and he slipped the usual tip into the porter's hand, and wishing him "good evening," went off.

"Well," he said to himself as he drove to Occleve House, "I should like to know what we went to that hotel for three days for! It wasn't because of the Dean's daughters nor yet for the foreign ladies, because he never spoke to any of them. Well, I'll buy a 'Special' and read about the murder."

Lord Penlyn walked on to Pall Mall, going very slowly and in an almost dazed state, and surprised several whom he met by his behaviour to them. Men whom he knew intimately he just nodded to instead of stopping to speak with for a moment, and some he did not seem to see at all. He was wondering what further particulars he would hear when he got to Cundall's club, and also when Smerdon would be back. That gentleman had started for Occleve Chase on Monday morning, but must by now have received a telegram Penlyn had sent him, telling him to return at once. In it he had cautiously, and without mentioning any names, given him to understand that their visitor of last Saturday had died suddenly, and he expected that he would return by the next train.

He had started off for Cundall's club, thinking to find out what was known, but, when he got there, he reflected that he could scarcely walk into a club, of which he was not a member, simply to make inquiries about even so important a subject as this. He could give no grounds for his eagerness to learn anything fresh, could not even say that he was particularly intimate with the dead man. Would it not look strange for him to be forcing his way in and making inquiries? Yes! and not only that, but it would draw attention on him, and it would be better to gather particulars elsewhere. He would go to his own club and find out what was known there.

So, looking very wan and miserable, he walked on to "Black's," and there he found the murder as much a subject of discussion as it was everywhere else. All the evening papers were full of it; the men who always profess to know something more than their fellows, whether it be with regard to a dark horse for a race, an understanding with Germany, or the full particulars of the next great divorce case—these men had heard all sorts of curious stories— that Cundall had a wife who had tracked him from the Tropics to slay him; that he had committed suicide because he was ruined; that he had been murdered by an outraged husband! There was nothing too far-fetched for these gentlemen!

Sifted down as the case was thoroughly by the papers, the facts that had come out, since first his body was discovered, amounted to this: He had been at his club late in the evening, and his brougham was waiting outside for him when the storm began. Then he had sent word down to his coachman to say that, as he had a letter to write, the carriage had better go home and he would take a cab later on. Other testimony, gathered by the papers, went on to show that he had sat on at his club, reading a little, and then going to a writing-table where he had sat some time; that when he had written his letter he went to a large arm-chair and read it over more than once, and then put a stamp on it, and, putting it in his pocket, still sat on and on, evidently thinking deeply. Two or three members said they had spoken to him, and one that he had told Cundall he did not seem very gay, but that he had replied in his usual pleasant manner, that he was very well, but had a good deal to occupy his mind. It was some time past two o'clock (the club, having a large number of Members of Parliament on its roll, was a late one) before the storm was over, and he rose to go. The hall-porter was apparently the last person who spoke to him alive, asking him if he should call a cab, but receiving for answer that, as the air was now so cool and fresh, he would walk home through the Park, it being so near to Grosvenor Place. The porter standing at the door of the club, himself to inhale the air, saw Mr. Cundall drop a letter in the pillar-box close by, and then go on. The only other person he noticed about, at that time, was a man who looked like a labourer, who was going the same way as Mr. Cundall. The sentries who had been on duty at, and around, St. James's Palace were also interrogated, and the one who had been outside Clarence House, stated that he distinctly remembered a gentleman answering to Mr. Cundall's description passing by him into the Park, at about a quarter to three. It was still raining slightly, and he had his umbrella up. He, too, saw the labourer, or mechanic, walking some fifteen yards behind him, and supposed he was going to his early work. From the time Mr. Cundall passed this man until the policeman found him dead, no one seemed to have seen him.

With the exception of the medical evidence, which stated that he had been stabbed to, and through, the heart by one swift, powerful blow, that must have caused instantaneous death, there was little more to be told. Judging from the state of the ground, there had been no struggle, a fact which would justify the idea that the murder had been planned and premeditated. The workman might have easily planned it himself in the time he followed him from outside his club to the time they were in the Park together, but he would have had to be provided with an extraordinarily long knife, such as workmen rarely carry. But, even had he not been the murderer, he must have seen the murder committed, since he was close at hand. It was, therefore, imperative that this man should be found. But to find one man in a city with four millions and a quarter of inhabitants was no easy task, especially when there was nothing by which to trace him. The sentry by whom he passed nearest thought he seemed to be a man of about five or six and twenty, with a brown moustache. But how many thousands of men were there in London to whom this description would apply!

Lord Penlyn sat there reading the "Specials," listening to the different opinions expressed, and particularly noting the revengeful utterances of men who had known Cundall. Their grief was loud, and strongly uttered, and it was evident that the regular police, or detective, force might be, if necessary, augmented by amateurs who would leave no stone unturned to try and get a clue to the murderer. Amongst others, he noticed one young man who was particularly grief-stricken, and who was constantly appealed to by those who surrounded him; and, on asking a fellow-member who he was, he learnt that he was a Mr. Stuart, the secretary of his dead brother. It happened that he had been brought into the club by a man who had known Cundall well.

"To-morrow," Penlyn heard him say, and he started as he heard it, "I am going to make a thorough investigation of all his papers. As far as I or his City agents know, he hadn't a relation in the world; but surely his correspondence must give us some idea of whom to communicate with. And, until this morning, I should have said he had not got an enemy in the world either."

"You think, then, that this dastardly murder is the work of an enemy, and not for mere robbery?" the gentleman asked who had brought him into the club.

"I am sure of it! As to the workman who is supposed to have done it—well, if he did do it, he was only a workman in disguise. No! he had some enemy, perhaps some one who owed him money, or whose path he had been enabled by his wealth to cross, and that is the man who killed him. And, by the grace of Heaven, I am going to find that man out."

Penlyn still sat there, and as he heard Stuart utter these words he felt upon what a precipice he stood. Suppose that, in the papers which were about to be ransacked, there should be any that proved that Walter Cundall was his eldest brother, and that he, Penlyn, had only learnt it two days before he was murdered. Would not everything point to him as the Cain who had slain his brother, and was he not making appearances worse against him by keeping silence? He must tell some one, he could keep the horrible secret no longer. And he must have the sympathy of some one dear to him; he would confide in Ida! Surely, she would not believe him to be the murderer of his own brother! Yes, he would go down to Belmont and tell her all. Better it should come from him than that Stuart should discover it, and publish it to the world.

"I hope you may find him out," several men said in answer to Stuart's exclamation. "The brute deserves something worse than hanging. If Cundall's murderer gets off, it is the wickedest thing that ever happened." Then one said: "Is there any clue likely to be got at through the wound?"

"No," Stuart answered, "I think not. Though the surgeon who has examined it says that it was made by no ordinary knife or dagger."

"What does he think it was, then?" they asked.

"He says the wound is more like those he has seen in the East. The dagger, he thinks, must have been semicircular and of a kind the Arabs often use, especially the Algerian Arabs."

"I never knew that!" one said; "but then I have never been to Algiers. Who has? Here, Penlyn, you were there once, weren't you?"

"Yes," Penlyn said, and his tongue seemed to cleave to the roof of his mouth as he uttered the words; "but I never saw or heard of a knife or dagger of that description."

Stuart looked at Lord Penlyn as he spoke, and noticed the faltering way in which he did so. Then, in a moment, the thought flashed into his mind that this was the man who had won the woman whom his generous friend and patron had loved. Could he—but no, the idea was ridiculous! He was the winner, Cundall the loser. Successful men had no reason to kill their unsuccessful rivals!

CHAPTER IX.

After a wretched night spent in tossing about his bed, in dreaming of the murdered man, and in lying awake wondering how he should break the news to Ida, Lord Penlyn rose with the determination of going down to Belmont. But when the valet brought him his bath he told him that Mr. Smerdon had arrived from Occleve Chase at six o'clock, and would meet him at breakfast. So, when he heard this, he dressed quickly and went to his friend.

"Good Heavens!" Philip said, when he saw him. "How ill you look! What is the matter?"

"Matter!" the other answered, "is there not matter enough to make me look ill? I have told you that Cundall is dead, and you know how he died."

"Yes, I know. But surely you must be aware of what it has freed you from."

"It has freed me from nothing. Read this; would that not have freed me equally as well?" and he handed him the letter that his brother had written a few hours before his death.

The other's face darkened as he read, and then he said:

"He was a man of noble impulses, but they were only impulses! Would you have ever felt sure while he lived that he might not alter his mind again at any moment?"

"Yes! He loved Ida, and I do not believe he was a man who would have ever loved another woman. I should have been safe in his hands."

Then they began to talk about the murder itself, and Smerdon asked who was suspected, or if any one was?

"No," Penlyn said, "no one is suspected—as yet. A labourer was seen following him on that night, and suspicion naturally falls on him, because, if he did not do it himself, he must have been close at hand, and would have helped him or given an alarm. There is only one road through the Park, which they must both have taken."

"Is there any trace of this man?"

"None whatever, up to last night. Meanwhile, his friend and secretary, Mr. Stuart, says that he is confident that the murder was committed by some one who had reason to wish him out of the way, and he is going through his papers to-day to see if any of them can throw any light on such an enemy."

"He cannot, I suppose, find anything that can do you any harm?"

"Supposing he finds those certificates he showed us?"

"Supposing he does! You are Lord Penlyn now, at any rate. And it would give you an opportunity of putting in a claim to his property. You are his heir, if he has left no will."

"His heir! To all his immense wealth?"

"Certainly."

"I shall never claim it, and I hope to God he has destroyed every proof of our relationship."

"Why?"

"Why! Because will not the fact that I held a position which belonged to him, and was the heir to all his money—of which I never thought till this moment—give the world cause for suspecting—?"

"What?"

"That I am his murderer."

"Nonsense! I suppose you could prove where you were at the time of his death?"

"No, I could not. I entered the hotel at two, but there was not a creature in the house awake. I could hear the porter's snores on the floor above, and there is not a living soul to prove whether I was in at three or not."

"Nor whether you were out! If they were all asleep, what evidence could they give on either side?"

"Even though there should be no evidence, how could I go through life with the knowledge that every one regarded me as his unproved murderer?"

"You look at the matter too seriously. To begin with, after that letter he wrote you, he would very likely destroy all proofs of his identity—"

"He had no chance. He was murdered, in all probability—indeed must have been—a quarter of an hour after he posted it in Pall Mall."

"He might have destroyed them before—when he made up his mind to write the letter."

"Certainly, he might have done so. But I am not going to depend upon his having destroyed them. This secret must be told by me, and I am going to Belmont to-day to tell it to Ida."

"You must be mad, I think!" Smerdon said, speaking almost angrily to him. "This secret, which only came to light a week ago, is now buried for ever, and, since he is dead, can never be brought up again. For what earthly reason should you tell Miss Raughton anything about it?"

"Because she ought to know," the other answered weakly. "It is only right that she should know."

"That you were not Lord Penlyn when you became engaged to her, but that you are now. And that Cundall being your brother, you must mourn him as a brother, and consequently your marriage must be postponed for at least a year. Is that what you mean?"

Lord Penlyn started. This had never entered into his head, and was certainly not what he would have meant or desired. Postponed for a year! when he was dying to make her his wife, when the very thought that his brother might step in and interrupt his marriage had been the cause of his brutality of speech to him. It had not been the impending loss of lands and position that had made him speak as he had done, he had told himself many times of late; it had been the fear of losing his beloved Ida. And, now that there was nothing to stand between them, he was himself about to place an obstacle in the way, an obstacle that should endure for at least a year. Smerdon was right, his quick mind had grasped what he would never have thought of—quite right! he would do well to say nothing about his relationship to the dead man. It is remarkable how easily we agree with those who show us the way to further our own ends!

"I never thought of that," he said, "and I could not bear it. After all," he went on weakly, "you are right! I do not see any necessity to say anything about it, and he himself forbade me to do so."

"There is only one thing, though," Smerdon said, "which is that, if you do not proclaim yourself his brother, I cannot see how you are to become possessed of his money."

"Don't think about it—I will never become possessed of it. It may go to any one but me, to some distant relative, if any can be found, or to the Crown, or whatever it is that takes a man's money when he is without kinsmen; but never to me. He was right when he said that I had been Jacob to his Esau all my life, but I will take no more from him, even though he is dead."

"Quixotic and ridiculous ideas!" Smerdon said. "In fact you and he had remarkably similar traits of character. Extremely quixotic, unless you have some strong reason for not claiming his millions. For instance, if *you had really murdered him* I could understand such a determination! But I suppose you did not do that!"

Lord Penlyn looked up and saw his friend's eyes fixed on him, with almost an air of mockery in them. Then he said:

"I want you to understand one thing, Philip. There must be no banter nor joking on this subject. Even though I must hold my peace for ever, I still regard it as an awful calamity that has fallen upon me. If I could do so, I would set every detective in London to work to try and find the man who killed him; indeed, if it were not for Ida's sake, I should proclaim myself his brother to-morrow."

"But for Ida's sake you will not do so?"

"For Ida's sake, and for the reason that I do not wish his money, I shall not; and more especially for the reason that you have shown me our marriage would be postponed if I did so. But never make such a remark again to me. You know me well enough to know that I am not of the stuff that murderers and fratricides are made of."

"I beg your pardon," Philip said; "of course I did not speak in earnest."

"On this subject we will, if you please, speak in nothing else but earnest. And, if you will help me with your advice, I shall be glad to have it."

"Let us go over the ground then," his friend said, "and consider carefully what you have to do. In the first place you have to look at the matter from two different points of view. One point is that you lose all claim to his money— yes, yes, I know," as Lord Penlyn made a gesture of contempt at the mention of the money—"all claim by keeping your secret. It is better, however, that you should so keep it. But, on the other hand, there is, of course, the chance— a remote one, a thousand to one chance, but still a chance—that he may have left some paper behind him which would prove your relationship to each other. In that case you would, of course, have no alternative but to acknowledge that you were brothers."

"And what would the world think of me then?"

"That you had simply done as he bade you, and kept the secret."

"It would think that I murdered him. It would be natural that the world should think so. He stood between me and everything, except Ida's love, and people might imagine that he possessed that too. And his murder, coming so soon after he disclosed himself to me, would make appearances against me doubly black."

"Who is to know when he disclosed himself to you? For aught the world knows, you might have been aware of your relationship for years."

"Then I was living a lie for years!"

"Do not wind round the subject so! And remember that, in very fact, you have done no harm. A week ago you did not know this secret."

"Well," Penlyn said, springing up from his chair, "things must take their course. If it comes out it must; if not, I shall never breathe a word to any one. Fate has cursed me with this trouble, I must bear it as best I can. The only thing I wish is that I had never gone to that hotel. That would also tell against me if anything was known."

"It was a pity, but it can't be helped. Now, go to Belmont, but be careful to hold your tongue."

Lord Penlyn did go to Belmont, having previously sent a telegram saying he was coming, and he travelled down in one of the special trains that was conveying a contingent of fashionable racing people to the second day at Ascot. But their joyousness, and the interest that they all took in the one absorbing subject, "What would win the Cup?" only made him feel doubly miserable. Why, he pondered, should these persons be so happy, when he was so wretched? And then, when they were tired of discussing the racing, they turned to the other great subject that was now agitating people's minds, the murder in St. James's Park. He listened with interest to all they had to say on that matter, and he found that, whatever the different opinions of the travellers in the carriage might be as to who the murderer was, they were all agreed as to the fact that it was no common murder committed for robbery, but one done for some more powerful reason.

"He stood in some one's light," one gentleman said, whom, from his appearance, Lord Penlyn took to be a barrister, "and that person has either removed him from this earth, or caused him to be removed. I should not like to be his heir, for on that man suspicion will undoubtedly fall, unless he can prove very clearly that he was miles away from London on Monday night."

Penlyn started as he heard these words. His heir! Then it would be on him that suspicion would fall if it was ever known that he was the heir; and, as he thought that, among his brother's papers, there might be something to prove that he was in such a position, a cold sweat broke out upon his forehead. How could he prove himself "miles away from London" on that night? Even the sleepy porter could not say at what time he returned to the hotel! Nothing, he reflected, could save him, if there was any document among the papers (that Stuart was probably ransacking by now) that would prove that he and Cundall were brothers.

He thought that, after all, it would be better he should tell Ida, and he made up his mind by the time he had arrived at the nearest station to Belmont, that he would do so. It would be far better that the information, startling as it might be, should come from him than from any other source. And while he was being driven swiftly over to Sir Paul's villa, he again told himself that it would be the best thing to do. Only, when he got to Belmont, he found his strength of mind begin to waver. The news of Cundall's dreadful death had had the effect of entirely breaking up the baronet's Ascot party. Every one there knew on what friendly terms the dead man had been both with father and daughter, and had been witness to the distress that both had felt at hearing the fatal tidings—Ida, indeed, had retired to her room, which she kept altogether; and consequently all the guests, with the exception of Miss Norris, had taken their departure. That young lady, whose heart was an extremely kind one, had announced that nothing should induce her to leave her dear friend until she had entirely recovered from the shock, and she had willingly abandoned the wearing of her pretty new frocks and had donned those more suited to a house of mourning; and she resigned herself to seeing no more racing, and to the loss of Mr. Fulke's agreeable conversation, and had devoted herself to administering to Ida. But, as Mr. Fulke and young Montagu had betaken themselves to an hotel not far off and had promised that they would look round before quitting the neighbourhood, she probably derived some consolation from knowing that she would see the former again.

"This is a dreadful affair, Penlyn!" the baronet said, when he received his future son-in-law in the pretty morning-room that Ida's own taste had decorated. "The shock has been bad enough to me, who looked upon Cundall as a dear friend, but it has perfectly crushed my poor girl. You know how much she liked him."

"Yes, I know," Penlyn answered, finding any reply difficult.

"Has she told you anything of what passed between them recently?" Sir

Paul asked.

"No," Penlyn said, "nothing." But the question told him that Ida had informed her father of the dead man's proposal to her.

"She will tell you, perhaps, when you see her. She intends coming down to you shortly." Then changing the subject, Sir Paul said: "She tells me you met the poor fellow at Lady Chesterton's ball. I suppose you did not see him after that, until—before his death?"

Lord Penlyn hesitated. He did not know what answer to give, for, though he had no desire to tell an untruth, how could he tell his questioner of the dreadful scenes that had occurred between them after that meeting at the ball?

Then he said, weakly: "Yes; I did see him again, at 'Black's.'"

"At 'Black's!'" Sir Paul exclaimed. "I did not know he was a member."

"Nor was he. Only, one night—Friday night—he was passing and I was there, and he dropped in."

"Oh!" Sir Paul said, "I thought you were the merest acquaintances."

And then he went on to discuss the murder, and to ask if anything further was known than what had appeared in the papers? And Penlyn told him that he knew of nothing further.

"I cannot understand the object of it," the baronet said. He had had but little opportunity of talking over the miserable end that had befallen his dead friend, and he was not averse now to discuss it with one who had also known him.

"I cannot understand," he went on, "how any creature, however destitute or vile, would have murdered him for his watch and the money he might chance to have about him. There must have been some powerful motive for the crime —some hidden enemy in the background of whom no one—perhaps, not even he himself—ever knew. I wonder who will inherit his enormous wealth?"

"Why?" Penlyn asked, and as he did so it seemed as though, once again, his heart would stop beating.

"Because I should think that that man would be in a difficult position— unless he can prove his utter absence from London at the time."

To Penlyn it appeared that everything pointed in men's minds to the same conclusion, that the heir of Walter Cundall was the guilty man. Every one was of the same opinion, Sir Paul, and the man going to Ascot who seemed like a lawyer; and, as he remembered, he had himself said the same thing to Smerdon. "What would the world think of him," he had asked, "if it should come to know that they were brothers, and that, being brothers, he was the inheritor of that vast fortune?" Yes, all thought alike, even to himself.

As these reflections passed through his mind it occurred to him that, after all, it would not be well for him to disclose to Ida the fact that he and Cundall were brothers—would she not know then that he was the heir, and might she not also then look upon him as the murderer? If that idea should ever come to her mind, she was lost to him for ever. No! Philip Smerdon was right; she must never learn of the fatal relationship between them.

"By-the-way," Sir Paul said, after a pause, "what on earth ever made you go to that hotel in town? Occleve House is comfortable enough, surely!"

Again Penlyn had to hesitate before answering, and again he had to equivocate. He had gone out of the house—that he thought was no longer his—with rage in his heart against the man who had come forward, as he supposed, to deprive him of everything he possessed; and never meaning to return to it, but to openly give to those whom it concerned his reasons for not doing so. But Cundall's murder had opened the way for him to return; the letter written on the night of his death had bidden Penlyn be everything he had hitherto been; and so he had gone back, with as honest a desire in his heart to obey his brother's behest as to reinstate himself.

But those two or three days at the hotel had surprised everybody, even to his valet and the house servants; and now Sir Paul was also asking for an explanation. What a web of falsehood and deceit he was weaving around him!

"There were some slight repairs to be done," he said, "and some alterations afterwards, so I had to go out."

"Then I wonder you did not come down here. The business you had to do might have been postponed."

He could make no answer to this, and it came as a relief to him when a servant announced that Miss Raughton would see him in the drawing-room. Only, he reflected as he went to her, if she, too, should question him as her father had done, he must go mad!

CHAPTER X.

When he saw the girl he loved so much rise wan and pale from the couch on which she had been seated waiting for his coming, his heart sank within him. How she must have suffered! he thought. What an awful blow Cundall's death must have been to her to make her look as she looked now, as she rose and stood before him!

"My darling Ida," he said, as he went towards her and took her in his arms and kissed her, "how ill and sad you look!"

She yielded to his embrace and returned his kiss, but it seemed to him as if her lips were cold and lifeless.

"Oh, Gervase!" she said, as she sank back to the couch wearily, "oh, Gervase! you do not know the horror that is upon me. And it is a double horror because at the time of his death, I knew of it."

"What!" he said, springing to his feet from the chair he had taken beside her. "What!"

"I saw it all," she said, looking at him with large distended eyes, eyes made doubly large by the hollows round them. "I saw it all, only—"

"Only what, Ida?"

"Only it was in a dream! A dream that I had, almost at the very hour he was treacherously stabbed to death."

As she spoke she leant forward a little towards him, with her eyes still distended; leant forward gazing into his face; and as she did so he felt the blood curdling in his veins!

"This," he said, trying to speak calmly, "is madness, a frenzy begotten of your state of mind at hearing—"

"It is no frenzy, no madness," she said, speaking in a strange, monotonous tone, and still with the intent gaze in her hazel eyes. "No, it is the fact. On that night—that night of death—he stood before me once again and bade me farewell for ever in this world, and then I saw—oh, my God!—his murderer spring upon him, and—"

"And that murderer was?" her lover interrupted, quivering with excitement.

"Unhappily, I do not know—not yet, at least, but I shall do so some day." She had risen now, and was standing before him pale and erect. The long white peignoir that she wore clung to her delicate, supple figure, making her look unusually tall; and she appeared to her lover like some ancient classic figure vowing vengeance on the guilty. As she stood thus, with a fixed look of certainty on her face, and prophesied that some day she should know the man who had done this deed, she might have been Cassandra come back to the world again.

"His face was shrouded," she went on, "as all murderers shroud their faces, I think; but his form I knew. I am thinking—I have thought and thought for hours by day and night—where I have seen that form before. And in some unexpected moment remembrance will come to me."

"Even though it does, I am afraid the remembrance will hardly bring the murderer to justice," Penlyn said. "A man can scarcely be convicted of a reality by a dream."

"No," she answered, "he cannot, I suppose. But it will tell me who that man is, and then—and then—"

"And then?" Penlyn interrupted.

"And then, if I can compass it, his life shall be subjected to such inspection, his every action of the past examined, every action of the present watched, that at last he shall stand discovered before the world!" She paused a moment, and again she looked fixedly at him, and then she said: "You are my future husband; do you know what I require of you before I become your wife?"

"Love and fidelity, Ida, is it not? And have you not that?"

"Yes," she answered, "but that fidelity must be tried by a strong test. You must go hand in hand with me in my search for his murderer, you must never falter in your determination to find him. Will you do this out of your love for me?"

"I will do it," Penlyn answered, "out of my love for you."

She held out her hand—cold as marble—to him, and he took it and kissed it. But as he did so, he muttered to himself: "If she could only know; if she could only know."

Again the impulse was on his lips to tell her of the strange relationship there was between him and the dead man, and again he let the impulse go. In the excitement of her mind would she not instantly conclude that he was the slayer of his dead brother, of the man who had suddenly come between him and everything he prized in the world? And, to support him in his weakness, was there not the letter of that dead brother enjoining secrecy? So he held his peace!

"I will do it," he said, "out of my love for you; but, forgive me, are you not taking an unusual interest in him, sad as his death was?"

"No," she answered. "No. He loved me; I was the only woman in the

65

world he loved—he told me so on the first night he returned to England. Only I had no love to give him in return; it was given to you. But I liked and respected him, and, since he came to me in my dream on that night of his death, it seems that on me should fall the task of finding the man who killed him."

"But what can you do, my poor Ida; you a delicately-nurtured girl, unused to anything but comfort and ease? How can you find out the man who killed him?"

"Only in one way, through you and by your help. I look to you to leave no stone unturned in your endeavours to find that man, to make yourself acquainted with Mr. Cundall's past life, to find out who his enemies, who his friends were; to discover some clue that shall point at last to the murderer."

"Yes," he said, in a dull, heavy voice. "Yes. That is what I must do."

"And when," she asked, "when will you begin? For God's sake lose no time; every hour that goes by may help that man to escape."

"I will lose no time," he answered almost methodically, and speaking in a dazed, uncertain way. Had it not been for her own excitement, she must have noticed with what little enthusiasm he agreed to her behest.

This behest had indeed staggered him! She had bidden him do the very thing of all others that he would least wish done, bidden him throw a light upon the past of the dead man, and find out all his enemies and friends. She had told him to do this, while there, in his own heart, was the knowledge of the long-kept secret that the dead man was his brother—the secret that the dead man had enjoined on him never to divulge. What was he to do? he asked himself. Which should he obey, the orders of his murdered brother, or the orders of his future wife? And Philip, too, had told him on no account to say anything of the story that had lately been revealed. Then, suddenly, he again determined that he would say nothing to her. It was a task beyond his power to appear to endeavour to track the murderer, or to give any orders on the subject; for since he must kelp the secret of their brotherhood, what right had he to show any interest in the finding of the murderer? Silence would, in every way, be best.

He rose after these reflections and told her that he was going back to London. And she also rose, and said:

"Yes, yes; go back at once! Lose no time, not a moment. Remember, you have promised. You will keep your promise, I know."

He kissed her, and muttered something that she took for words of assent, and prepared to leave her.

"You will feel better soon, dearest, and happier, I hope. This shock will pass away in time."

"It will pass away," she answered, "when you bring me news that the murderer is discovered, or that you have found out some clue to him. It will begin to pass away when I hear that you have found out what enemies he had."

"It is not known that he ever had any enemies," Penlyn said, as he stood holding her cold hand in his. "He was not a man to make enemies, I should think."

"He must have had some," she said, "or one at least—the one who slew him." She paused, and gazed out of the open window by which they were standing, gazed out for some moments; and he wondered what she was thinking of now in connection with him. Then she turned to him again and said:

"Do you think you could find out if he had any relatives?" and he could not repress a slight start as she asked him this, though she did not perceive it. "I never heard him say that he had any, but he may have had. I should like to know."

"Why, Ida?"

"Because—because—oh, I do not know!—my brain is in a whirl. But—if —if you should find out that he had any relations, then I should like to know."

And again he asked: "Why, Ida?"

"I would stand face to face with them, if they were men," she answered, speaking in a low tone of voice that almost appalled him, "and look carefully at them to see if they, or one of those relations, bore any resemblance to the shrouded figure that sprang upon him in my dream."

"If there are any such they will, perhaps, be heard of," he said; but as he spoke he prayed inwardly that she might never know of his relationship to Cundall. If she ever learnt that, would she not look to see if he bore any resemblance to that dark figure of her dream? He was committed to silence— to silence not without shame, alas!—for ever now, and he shuddered as he acknowledged this to himself. Once more he bade her farewell, promising to come back soon, and then he left her.

"She looks dreadfully ill and overcome by this sad calamity," he said to Sir Paul before he also parted with him. "I hope she will not let it weigh too much upon her mind."

"She cannot help it doing so, poor girl," the baronet said. "Of course she told you that Cundall proposed to her on the night of his return, not knowing that she had become engaged to you."

"She told me that he loved her, and that she learnt of his love on that night for the first time," Penlyn answered.

"Yes, that was the case," Sir Paul said. "It was at Lady Chesterton's ball that he proposed to her."

They talked for some little time further on the desire she had expressed to see the murderer brought to justice, and Penlyn said he feared she was exciting herself too much over the idea.

"Yes, I am afraid so," Sir Paul said; "yet, I suppose, the wish is natural. She looks upon herself as, in some way, the person to whom his death was first made known, and seems to think it is her duty to try and aid in the discovery of the man who killed him. Of course, it is impossible; and she can do nothing, though she has begged me to try everything in my power to assist in finding his assassin. I would do so willingly, for I admired Cundall's character very much; but there is also nothing I could do that the police cannot do better."

"Of course not, but still her wish is natural," Penlyn said, and then he said "Good-bye" to Sir Paul also, and went back to London.

As he sat in the train on the return journey, he wondered what fresh trouble and sorrow there could possibly be in store for him over the miserable events of the past week, and he also wondered if he ever again would know peace upon this earth! It was impossible to help looking back to a short month ago, to the time before that discovery had been made at the inn at Le Vocq, and to remembering how happy he had been then, how everything in this world had seemed to smile upon him. He had been happy in his love for Ida, happy in the position he held in the eyes of men, happy without any alloy to his happiness. And then, from the moment when he had found that there was another son of his father in the world, how all the brightness of his life had changed! First had come the knowledge of that brother alive somewhere, whom, thinking he was poor and outcast, he had pitied; then the revelation that that brother, far from being the abject creature he imagined, was in actual fact the rightful owner of the position he usurped; and then the horror and the misery of the cruelly barbarous death that brother had been put to, directly after revealing himself in his true light. And, as horrible almost as all else were, the lies, and the secrecy, and the duplicities with which he had environed himself, in the hopes of shielding everything from the eyes of the world. Lies, and secrecies, and duplicities practised by him, who had once regarded truth and openness as the first attributes of a man!

And there was one other thing that struck deeply to his heart; the bitter wickedness of a man, with such nobility of nature as his brother had shown, being cruelly stabbed to death. His life had been one long abnegation of what should have been his, a resignation of the honour of his birthright, so that he, who had taken his place, should never be cast out of it; an abnegation that had been crowned by an almost sublime act, the act of forcing himself to witness the happiness of the one, who had taken so much from him, with the woman he had long loved. For, that he had determined to resign all hopes of her, there was, after the letter he had written, no doubt. And, as he thought of all the unselfishness of that brother's nature, and of his awful death, the tears flowed to his eyes, and, being alone, he buried his head in his hands and wept as he had wept once before. "If I could call him back again," he said to himself, "if I could once more see him stand before me alive and well, I would cheerfully go out a beggar into the world. But it cannot be, and I must bear the lot that has fallen on me as best I can."

He reached his house early in the evening, and the footman handed him a letter that had been left by a messenger but a short time before. It ran as follows.

"GROSVENOR PLACE, *June 12th*, 188-

"MY LORD,

"In searching through the papers of my late employer, Mr. Walter Cundall, I have come across a will made by him three years ago. By it, the whole of his fortune and estates are left to you, your names and title being carefully described. I have placed the will in the hands of Mr. Fordyce, Mr. Cundall's solicitor, from whom you will doubtless hear shortly.

"Your obedient Servant,

"A. STUART.

"The Rt. Hon. Viscount Penlyn."

That was all; without one word of explanation or of surprise at the manner in which Walter Cundall's vast wealth had been bequeathed.

Lord Penlyn crushed the letter in his hand when he had read it, and, as he threw himself into a chair, he moaned, "Everything must be known, everything discovered; there is no help for it! What will Ida think of me now? Why did I not tell her to-day? Why did I not tell her?"

CHAPTER XI.

That night he did not go to bed at all, but paced his room or sat buried in his deep chair, wondering what the morrow would bring forth and how he should best meet the questions that would be put to him. Smerdon was gone again to Occleve Chase, so he could take no counsel from him; and, in a way, he was almost glad that he had gone, for he did not know that he should be inclined now to follow any advice his friend might give him. He thought he knew what that advice would be—that he should pretend utter ignorance as to the reasons Cundall might have had for making him the inheritor of all his vast wealth, and on no account to acknowledge the brotherhood between them. But he told himself that, even had Smerdon been there to give such advice, it would not have been acceptable; that he would not have followed it.

As hour after hour went by and the night became far advanced, the young man made up his mind determinately that, henceforth, all subterfuge and secrecy should be abandoned, that there should be no more holding back of the truth, and that, when he was asked if he could give any reason why he should have been made the heir to the stupendous fortune of a man who was almost a stranger to him, he would boldly announce that it had been so left to him because he and Cundall were the sons of one father.

"The world," he said sadly to himself, "may look upon me as the man who killed him in the Park, and will look upon me as having for years occupied a false position; but it must do so if it chooses. I cannot go on living this life of deception any longer. No! Not even though Ida herself should cast me off." But he thought that though he might bear the world's condemnation, he did not know how he would sustain the loss of her love. Still, the truth should be told even though he should lose her by so telling it; even though the whole world should point to him as a fratricide!

He had wavered for many days now as to what course he should take, had had impulses to speak out and acknowledge the secret of his and his brother's life, had been swayed by Smerdon's arguments and by the letter he had received at the hotel, but now there was to be no more wavering; all was to be told. And, if there was any one who had the right to ask why he had not spoken earlier, that very letter would be sufficient justification of his silence. It was about midday that, as he was seated in his study writing a long letter to Smerdon explaining exactly what he had now taken the determination of doing, the footman entered with two cards on which were the names of "Mr. Fordyce, Paper Buildings," and "Mr. A. Stuart."

"The gentlemen wish to know if your lordship can receive them?" the man asked.

"Yes," Penlyn answered, "I have been expecting a visit from them. Show them in."

They came in together, Mr. Fordyce introducing himself as the solicitor of the late Mr. Cundall, and Mr. Stuart bowing gravely. Then Lord Penlyn motioned to them both to be seated.

"I received your letter last night," he said to the secretary, "and, although I may tell you at once that there were, perhaps, reasons why Mr. Cundall should have left me his property, I was still considerably astonished at hearing he had done so."

"Reasons, my lord!" Mr. Fordyce said, looking up from a bundle of papers which he had taken from his pocket and was beginning to untie. "Reasons! What reasons, may I ask?"

The lawyer, who from his accent was evidently a Scotch-man, was an elderly man, with a hard, unsympathetic face, and it became instantly apparent to Penlyn that, with this man, there must not be the slightest hesitation on his part in anything he said, nor must anything but the plainest truth be spoken. Well! that was what he had made up his mind should be done, and he was glad as he watched Mr. Fordyce's face that he had so decided.

"The reason," he answered, looking straight at both of them, "is that he and I were brothers."

"Brothers!" they both exclaimed together, while Stuart fixed his eyes upon him with an incredulous look, though in it there was something else besides incredulity, a look of suspicion and dislike.

"This is a strange story, Lord Penlyn," the lawyer said after a moment.

"Yes," the other answered. "And you will perhaps think it still more strange when I tell you that I myself did not know of it until a week ago."

"Not until a week ago!" Stuart said. "Then you could have learnt of your relationship only two or three days before he was murdered?"

"That is the case," Penlyn said.

"I think, Lord Penlyn," Mr. Fordyce said, "that, as the late Mr. Cundall's solicitor, and the person who will, by his will, have a great deal to do with the administration of his fortune, you should give me some particulars as to the relationship that you say he and you stood in to one another."

"If Lord Penlyn intends to do so, and wishes it, I will leave the house," Stuart said, still speaking in a cold, unsympathetic voice.

"By no means," Penlyn said. "It will be best that you both should hear all that I know."

Then he told them, very faithfully, everything that had passed between him and Walter Cundall, from the night on which he had come to Black's Club, and they had had their first interview in the Park, down to the letter that had been written on the night of the murder. Nor did he omit to tell them it was only a month previous to Cundall's disclosing himself, that he and Philip Smerdon had made the strange discovery at Le Vocq that his father, to all appearances, had had a previous wife, and had, also, to all appearances, left an elder son behind him. Only, he said, it had seemed a certainty to him and his friend that the lady was not actually his wife, and that the child was not his lawful son. If there was anything he did not think it necessary to tell them it was the violence of his behaviour to Cundall at the interview they had had in that very room, and the curse he had hurled after him when he was gone, and the wish that "he was dead." That curse and that wish, which had been fulfilled so terribly soon after their expression, had weighed heavily on his heart ever since the night of the murder; he could not repeat it now to these men.

"It is the strangest story I ever heard," Mr. Fordyce said. "The very strangest! And, as we have found no certificates of either his mother's marriage or his own birth, we must conclude that he destroyed them. But the letter that you have shown us, which he wrote to you, is sufficient proof of your relationship. Though, of course, as he has named you fully and perfectly in the will there would be no need of any proof of your relationship."

"The man," Stuart said quietly, "who murdered him, also stole his watch and pocket-book, probably with the idea of making it look like a common murder for robbery. The certificates were perhaps in that pocket-book!"

"Do you not think it *was* a common murder for robbery?" Lord Penlyn asked him.

"No, I do not," Stuart answered, looking him straight in the face. "There was a reason for it!

"What reason?"

"That, the murderer knows best."

It was impossible for Penlyn to disguise from himself the fact that this young man had formed the opinion in his mind that he was the murderer. His manner, his utter tone of contempt when speaking to him, were all enough to show in what light he stood in Stuart's eyes.

"I understand you," he said quietly.

Stuart took no notice of the remark, but he turned to Mr. Fordyce and said: "Did it not seem strange to you that Lord Penlyn should have been made the heir, when you drew the will?"

"I did not draw it," Mr. Fordyce said, "or I should in all probability have made some inquiries—though, as a matter of fact, it was no business of mine to whom he left his money. As I see there is one Spanish name as a witness, it was probably drawn by an English lawyer in Honduras, and executed there."

"Since it appears that I am his heir," Lord Penlyn said, "I should wish to see the will. Have you it with you?"

"Yes," Mr. Fordyce said, producing the will from his bundle of papers, and handing it to him, "it is here."

The young man took it from the lawyer, and spreading it out before him, read it carefully. The perusal did not take long, for it was of the shortest possible description, simply stating that the whole of everything he possessed was given and bequeathed by him to "Gervase, Courteney, St. John, Occleve, Viscount Penlyn, in the Peerage of Great Britain, of Occleve House, London, and Occleve Chase, Westshire." With the exception that the bequest was enveloped in the usual phraseology of lawyers, it might have been drawn up by his brother's own hand, so clear and simple was it. And it was perfectly regular, both in the signature of the testator and the witnesses.

The two men watched him as he bent over the will and read it, the lawyer looking at him from under his thick, bushy eyebrows, and Mr. Stuart with a fixed glance that he never took off his face; and as they so watched him they noticed that his eyes were filled with tears he could not repress. He passed his hand across them once to wipe the tears away, but they came again; and, when he folded up the document and gave it back to Mr. Fordyce, they were welling over from his eyelids.

"I saw him but once after I knew he was my brother," he said; "and I had very little acquaintance with him before then; but now that I have learnt how whole-souled and unselfish he was, and how he resigned everything that was dear to him for my sake, I cannot but lament his sad life and dreadful end. You must forgive my weakness."

"It does you honour, my lord," the lawyer said, speaking in a softer tone than he had yet used; "and he well deserved that you should mourn him. He had a very noble nature."

"If you really feel his loss, if you feel it as much as I do, who owed much to him," Stuart said, "you will join me in trying to track his murderer. That will be the most sincere mourning you can give him;" and he, too, spoke now in a less bitter tone.

"I promised, yesterday, the woman whom we both loved that I would leave no stone unturned to find that man; I need take no fresh vows now. But what clue is there to show us who it was that killed him?"

For a moment neither of the others answered. He had been dead now for four days, the inquest had been held yesterday, and he was to be buried on the following day; yet through all those proceedings this man who was his kinsman, this man for whom he had exhibited the tenderest love and unselfishness, had made no sign, had not even come forward to see to the disposal of his remains. Stuart asked himself what explanation could be given of this, and, finding no answer in his own mind, he plainly asked Lord Penlyn if he himself could give any.

"Yes," he answered; "yes, I can. He had charged me in that letter that I should never make known what our positions were; charged me when he could have had no idea of death overtaking him; and I thought that I should best be consulting his wishes by keeping silence when he was dead. And I tell you both frankly that, had it not been for this will—the existence of which I never dreamed of—I never should have spoken, never have proclaimed our relationship. For the sake of my future wife, as well as to obey him, I should not have done so. He was dead, and no good could have been done by speaking."

"It will lead to your conduct being much misconstrued by the world," Mr. Fordyce said. "It will not understand your silence."

"Must everything be made public?" Penlyn asked.

"More or less. One cannot suppress a will dealing with over two millions worth of property. Even though you were willing to destroy it and forfeit your inheritance, it could not be done. If Mr. Stuart and I allowed such a thing as that, we should become criminals."

"Well, so be it! the public must think what they like of me—at least until the murderer is discovered." Then he asked again: "But what clue is there to help us to find him?"

"None that we know of, as yet," Stuart said. "The verdict at the Coroner's Inquest yesterday was, 'Wilful murder against some person or persons unknown,' and the police stated that, up to now, they could not say that they suspected any one. There is absolutely no clue!"

"I suppose," Mr. Fordyce said, with a speculative air, "those Spanish letters will not furnish any, when translated.'"

"What Spanish letters?" Penlyn asked. "If you have any, let me see them, I am acquainted with the language."

"Is *Corot* a man's or a woman's name?" Mr. Fordyce asked, as he again untied his bundle of papers.

"Neither, that I know of," Penlyn answered. "It is more likely, I should think, to be a pet, or nickname. Why do you ask?"

"I found these three letters amongst others in his desk," Stuart said, taking them from Mr. Fordyce and handing them to Lord Penlyn, "and I should not have had my attention attracted to them more than to any others out of the mass of foreign correspondence there was, had it not been for the marginal notes in Mr. Cundall's handwriting. Do you see them?"

"Yes," he answered. "Yes. I see written on one, '*Sent C 500 dols.*,' on another, '*Sent 2,000 Escudos*,' and on the third again, '*Sent C 500 dols.*'"

"What do the letters say?" they both asked.

"I will read them."

He did so carefully, and then he turned round and said:

"They are all from some man signing himself *Corot*, and dating from Puerto Cortes, who seems to think he had, or, perhaps, really had, since money was sent, some claim upon him. In the first one he says none has been forthcoming for a long while, and that, though he does not want for himself, some woman, whom he calls *Juanna*, is ill and requires luxuries. He finishes his letter with, 'Yours ever devotedly.' In the second he writes more strongly, says that *Juanna* is dying, and that, as she has committed no fault, he insists upon having money. After this the largest sum was sent."

"And the third?" they both asked.

"The third is more important. It says *Juanna* is dead, that he is going to England on business, and that, as he has heard Cundall is also about to set out for that country, he will see him there, as he cannot cross Honduras to do so. And he finishes his letter by saying: 'Do not, however, think that her death relieves you from your liability to me. Justice, and the vile injuries done to us, make it imperative on you to provide for me for ever out of your evilly-acquired wealth. This justice I will have, and you know I am one who will not hesitate to enforce my rights. Remember how I served *José*, and beware.'"

"This is a faithful translation?" Stuart asked.

"Take it to an interpreter, as you doubt me?" Penlyn said.

"I do not doubt you, Lord Penlyn," the other replied, "and I beg your pardon for this and any other suspicions I may have shown. Will you forgive me?"

"Yes," Penlyn said, and he held out his hand to the other, and Stuart took it.

"If this man is in England," Mr. Fordyce said, "and we could only find him out, and also discover what his movements have been, we should, perhaps, be very near the murderer."

"Every detective in London shall be set to work to-night, especially those who understand foreigners and their habits, to find him if he is here. And if he is, he will have to give a very full account of himself before he finds himself free," Stuart said.

CHAPTER XII.

The conversation between the three was, necessarily, of so lengthy a nature, that Lord Penlyn desired them to partake of some luncheon, which invitation they accepted. While it was proceeding, they continued to discuss fully all the extraordinary circumstances of which they had any knowledge in connection with the murder of Walter Cundall, and also of the position in which Penlyn now found himself.

"Of course, it is no use trying to disguise the fact, my lord," the lawyer said, "that this strange will in your favour will be the subject of much discussion. The only thing we have to do now is to think how much need be made public. Your inheritance of his money—even to a nobleman in your position—is a matter of importance, and will cause a great deal of remark."

"Of course, I understand that," Penlyn answered. "But you say we have to think of 'how much' need be made public. What part of this unhappy story is there that you imagine need not be known?"

Mr. Fordyce thought a moment, with his bushy eyebrows deeply knitted, then he said:

"I do not see why any one need be told of the relationship existing between you. It is no one's business after all; and it was evidently his wish that, for your sake, it should never be known."

"Naturally," Penlyn replied, "I do not want my affairs told to every one, and made a subject of universal gossip; but then, what reason is to be given for his having left me all his money?"

"It might be hinted that you were connections, though distant ones," Mr. Fordyce said.

"Would it not appear strange that, in such circumstances, we knew so little of one another?"

"Yes," the lawyer said, "unless it were said that you were only recently acquainted with the fact."

"But the will is dated three years ago!" Stuart remarked. "Then I scarcely know what to suggest," Mr. Fordyce said.

They talked it over and over again, but they could arrive at no determination; and at last it was resolved that the best thing would be to let matters take their course. No announcement would be publicly made, and though, of course, it would, eventually leak out that Lord Penlyn was Walter Cundall's heir, the world would have to put its own construction upon the fact. Or again, other men had before now made eccentric wills, taking sudden fancies to people who were strangers to them and leaving them all their money. It would be best that Walter Cundall's will should also come to be regarded in that category.

"After all," Stuart said, "you were acquaintances, and mixed in the same circle. Even the fact that you both loved the same woman goes for something, and that must be sufficient for those who take any interest in the matter."

He had come into the house with innumerable suspicions against Lord Penlyn, suspicions aroused by his being the inheritor of Cundall's property, and also by the fact that he and the dead man had both loved the same woman, and with a strange feeling in his heart that, when he stood before him, he would stand before a murderer. He had also remembered that conversation in the club about the peculiarity of the dagger, or knife, with which Cundall must have been slain, and his recollection of the hesitating way in which Penlyn had answered, had added to his suspicions. But, when he had seen the genuine tears of sorrow that had been shed over the will, those suspicions vanished, and he told himself that it was not in this man that the murderer would be found. And, if this new-formed idea had required any strengthening, it would have received it when those importunate and threatening letters had been read from the unknown person signing himself, *Corot*. There was the man, who, if in England, must be found at all costs. But how to find him was the question.

"There is one to whom I must, at least, disclose my relationship with Walter," Penlyn said, and they both noticed that, for the first time, he spoke of his brother by his Christian name. "I must tell Miss Raughton the position we stood in to one another."

Stuart, with feelings of a very different nature now in his heart from those with which he had first regarded him, asked him if he thought it was wise to do so? Would she not think that, standing in the position of his affianced wife and having also been beloved by his brother, she should have been the first to be told of the bond between them?

"It may not be wise," Penlyn said sadly, and with a weary look upon his face, "and it may be that she will think I have deceived her—as, unhappily, I have done by my silence—but still I must tell her. With her, at least, there must be nothing more suppressed."

Then he told them of the strange dream that she had had (even mentioning that she had said she could recognise the form, if not the face, of the man who sprang upon him), and of the vow she had made him take to endeavour to discover the murderer.

"If dreams were of the slightest importance, which they are not," Mr. Fordyce said, "this one would go to prove that *Corot* is not the murderer, since it is hardly likely that she has ever known him. Still, it is a strange coincidence that she should have dreamt of his death on the very night that it took place."

"The idea of knowing the form, or figure, of the man is nothing," Stuart said. "If there was any likelihood of there being anything in that, it would also be the case that we should have to look upon Lady Chesterton's conservatory as the spot where it happened, as it was there she dreamt she saw him. But we know that he was killed in St. James' Park."

"If the detectives can only discover this man *Corot*," Penlyn said, "we might find out what he was doing on that night."

"If they cannot find him," Stuart said, "it shall not be for the want of being paid to look for him."

"I would give every farthing of the fortune my brother has left me to discover him, or to find the real assassin!" Penlyn said.

They discussed, after this, the way in which the information that had come into their possession, from the three letters written in Spanish, should be conveyed to the detectives, and Stuart arranged to take the matter into his hands.

"Leave it to me," he said, "I happen to know two or three of them; in fact, I have already communicated with Dobson, who understands a great deal about foreigners. He has done all the big extradition cases for a long while, and knows the exact spots in which men of different nationalities are to be found. If *Corot* is in London, Dobson, or one of his men, will be sure to discover him."

"And you think I had better not appear in the matter at all?" Penlyn asked, appealing to both of them.

"Not at present, certainly," Mr. Fordyce said; "as Mr. Stuart is at present acting in it, it had better be left to him. Mr. Cundall's agents in the City have placed everything in his hands, and I suppose you, as his heir, will have no objection to do so also."

"I shall be extremely grateful to Mr. Stuart if he will hold the same position towards me that he filled with my brother," Penlyn said; "and if he wants any assistance, my friend and secretary, Mr. Smerdon, will be happy to render it him."

"I will do all I can," Stuart said quietly, "to assist you, both in regard to his affairs and to finding the guilty man if possible."

Then Lord Penlyn made a suggestion that his own lawyer, Mr. Bell, should also be brought into communication with Mr. Fordyce and Stuart, and the former said that he would call upon him the next day.

"There will then be five of us interested in finding the assassin," Penlyn said, "for I am quite sure that both Mr. Bell and Philip Smerdon will go hand in hand with us in this search. Surely amongst us, and with the aid of the detectives, who ought to work well for the reward I will pay them, we shall succeed in tracking him."

"I hope to God we shall!" Stuart said, and Penlyn solemnly exclaimed, "Amen!"

They were about to separate now, after an interview that had lasted for some hours, when Penlyn said:

"To-morrow is the day of his funeral. If it were possible—if you think that

I could do so, I should wish to be present at it."

The others thought a moment, Stuart looking at Mr. Fordyce as though waiting for him to answer this suggestion, but, instead of doing so, he only said: "What do you think, Mr. Stuart?"

Stuart still hesitated, and seemed to be pondering deeply, and then he said:

"I think, if it will not be too great a denial to you, if you will not feel that you are failing in the last duty you can pay him, you should remain away. You could only go as chief mourner if you go at all, and that will render you too conspicuous, and would set every tongue in London wagging. Can you resign yourself to staying away?"

"I must resign myself, I suppose," the other answered. "Perhaps, too, it is better I should do so; for, when I should see his coffin being lowered into its grave, the memory of his nobility and unselfishness, and his cruel end, would come back to me with such force that I fear I should no longer be master of myself."

So Lord Penlyn did not see the last of his brother's remains; and Mr. Stuart, Mr. Fordyce, and two of his agents made up the list of his mourners. But behind the carriage that conveyed them, came countless other carriages belonging to men and women who had known and liked the dead man, and in some cases their owners were in them; amongst others Sir Paul Raughton being in his. The wreaths of flowers that were piled above his coffin also came from scores of friends, and afforded great interest to the enormous mob that followed the victim's funeral, and made a decorous holiday of the occasion. It is not often that a millionaire is stabbed to death in London by an unknown hand; and many of those, who had read with intense excitement of the murder, determined to see the last obsequies of the victim. Amongst those wreaths were two formed of splendid white roses, one of which bore the words worked into it, "We shall meet again" and the initial letter "I," and another the words, "I remember" followed by the letter "G."

And late that night, as the time was, fast approaching for the cemetery to be closed, Lord Penlyn walked swiftly up the path leading to the new-made grave, and, seeing that there was no one near, knelt down and prayed silently by it. Then he whispered, "I will never rest until you are avenged. If you can hear my vow in heaven, hear me now swear this." And, taking a handful of the mould from the grave, he wrapped it in his handkerchief, and passed out again into the world.

CHAPTER XIII.

The Hôtel et Café Restaurant de Lepanto is one of those many places near, and in the neighbourhood of, Leicester Square, where foreigners delight to sojourn when in London. Not first-class foreigners, perhaps, or, at least, not foreigners of large means, but generally such as come to London to transact business that occupies them for a short time. As a rule, this establishment is patronised by Spanish and Portuguese gentlemen of a commercial status, persons who, more often than not, are connected with the wine trade of those countries; and it is also frequented by singers and dancers and other *artistes* who may find themselves—by what they regard as a stroke of fortune— fulfilling an engagement in our Metropolis. To them, the Hôtel Lepanto is a congenial abode, a spot where they can eat of the oily and garlic-flavoured dishes partaken of with so much relish when at home in Madrid, Lisbon, Seville, or Granada, and here they can converse in their own tongues with each other and with Diaz Zarates, the Spanish landlord of the house, to whom half-a-dozen Southern languages and many *patois* are known.

The hotel seems to exist entirely for the people of these countries, since into it no Frenchman, nor Italian, nor German ever comes; they have their own hostelries of an equally, to them, agreeable nature in other streets in the neighbourhood. So these Southerners, with the dark eyes, and coal-black hair, and brown skin, have the little dining-room with the dirty fly-blown paper, and the almost as dirty table-covers and curtains, all to themselves; and into it —or to the passage with the three chairs and the marble-table where, as often as not, the Señors and Señoras sit and smoke their cigarettes for hours together, in preference to doing so in the dining-room—no one of another nation intrudes. If, not having Spanish or Portuguese blood in his veins, there ever is any one who does so intrude, it is generally some Englishman of a rashly speculative nature, who wants to try a Spanish dinner and see what it is like, and who, having done so, never wants to try another.

And sometimes, as has been the case of late, much to the disgust of Diaz Zarates, an English detective has made his appearance, and, under the guise of one of the above speculative individuals essaying an Iberian meal, has endeavoured to worm secrets out of him about his patrons and guests. To the disgust of Diaz Zarates of late, because he knows perfectly well who Dobson is (although that astute individual is not aware of the landlord's knowledge of his calling), and because, honestly, he has never heard of any one bearing the name of *Corot* in his life.

And it is of such a person with that name, that Dobson has been making little inquiries whenever he has dropped in to try a Spanish luncheon or a Spanish dinner.

Seated, a few days after the murder of Walter Cundall, on one of the three chairs in the passage, and meditatively smoking cigarettes out of which, as is the case with Spanish-made ones, the tobacco would frequently fall in a lighted mass on the marble table, was Señor Miguel Guffanta, as he was inscribed in Diaz's books. Had the Señor been as carefully washed as the upper classes of Spaniards usually are, had his linen been as white and clean as the linen usually worn by the upper classes of Spaniards, and, had he been freshly shaved, he would, in all probability have presented the appearance of a fine, handsome man. But he had come downstairs this morning to smoke his cigarette, without troubling to make his toilette, putting on his yesterday's shirt, and going through no ablutionary process at all, and with a thick, heavy stubble of twenty-four hours' growth upon his cheeks and chin. Still, with all this carelessness, Señor Miguel Guffanta was a handsome man. He had a dark, Moorish-looking face, the lines of which were very regular, he had large luminous eyes that, when he chose, he could open to an enormous extent, and coal-black hair that curled thickly over his head. His frame was a powerful one; his height being considerable and his chest broad and deep, and his long, sinewy, brown hands looked as though their grasp would be a grasp of iron, if put to their utmost strength. In age he was about thirty-eight or forty, but he looked younger, because no single gray hair had appeared either in his luxurious locks or in his long, black moustache. As he sat there, taking fresh cigarette-papers from his pocket, and, when he had put some dry, dusty tobacco into them, twisting both ends up, and smoking them while he gazed meditatively either at the ceiling of the passage, or into the species of horse-box that was designated as the "bureau," a stranger might have wondered what brought the Señor there. Unkempt as he was this morning, there was something about him, either in the easy grace of his figure, or in the contemptuous, almost haughty, look in his face, that proclaimed instantly that this was not a man accustomed to soliciting orders for wine, or to appearing in Spanish ballets or choruses, or of, in any way, ministering to other people's amusement.

As he still sat there thinking and smoking, the landlord came down the passage, and bowing and wishing him "Good morning" in Spanish, entered his box, and proceeded to make some entries in his books. The Señor nodded in return, and then made another cigarette and went on with his meditations; but, when that one was smoked through, he rose and leaned against the door-post of the bureau, and addressed Zarates.

"And have any more guests arrived since last night," he asked, "and is the hotel yet full?"

"No more, Señor, no more as yet," the landlord answered him. "*Dios!* but there is little business doing now."

"That is not well! And he who loves so much our Spanish luncheons and dinners, our good friend Dobson (he pronounced the name, Dobesoon) with the heavy, fat face and the big beard—what of him?"

"He is a pig, a fool!" Diaz said, as he ran an unclean finger up a column of accounts. "He believes me not when I tell him that of his accursed *Corot* I know nothing, and that I believe no such man is in London."

The Señor laughed gently to himself at this answer, and then he said: "And he has not yet found him?"

"*Dios!* found him, no! Of that name I never heard before, no, never! There is no such name!"

"For what does he say he wishes to see this *Corot?* Is it that he has a legacy to give him, or has he committed a crime for which this fat man, this heavy Alguazil, wants to arrest him?"

"*Quien sabé!* He says he has a little friendly question to ask him, that is all. He says if he could see him for one moment, he would tell him all he wants to know. And then he says he must find him. But I do not think now he will ever find him."

"Nor do I," the Señor said. Then he looked up at the clock, and, seeing it was past twelve, went to his room, saying that it was time he prepared himself for the day.

But when he reached that apartment, which was a small room on the second floor, that looked out on to the back windows of the street that ran parallel with the one in which the Hôtel Lepanto was situated, it did not seem as if those preparations stood in any great need of hurry. The inevitable cigarette-papers were again produced and the dusty tobacco, and the Señor, throwing himself into the arm-chair that stood in the corner of the room, again gave himself up to meditation.

"*Corot*," he said to himself, "*Corot*. How is it that that man has ever heard the name—what does he know about it, why should he want to find him? I thought that, outside Los Torros and Puerto Cortes, that name had never been heard. Walter knew it, and Juanna knew it, and I knew it, but of others there was no one alive who knew it. Yet here, is this big, stupid man, in this big, stupid city (where—*por Dios!* one may be stabbed to death and none find the slayer), with the name upon his lips. How has he ever heard it, how has he ever known of it?"

He could find no answer to these questions which he asked himself, and gradually his thoughts went off into another train.

"So, after all," he continued, "his name was not Cundall but Occleve, and he it was who was this lord, this Penlyn, though that other bears the name. And he, who inherited all that wealth from the old man, had no right to it, no not so much right as Juanna—poor Juanna!—and I had. And now he is gone, and it is with the living that I have to do. Well, it shall be done, and by my father's blood the reckoning shall be a heavy one if this lord does not clear himself!"

He rose from his seat, and, going to a cupboard, took from it a suit of clothes of good, dark material, and after brushing them carefully, laid them out upon the bed. From a shelf in it he took out a very good silk hat, which he also brushed, and a pair of nearly new gloves. Then he rang the bell, and bade the servant who answered it bring him sufficient hot water for shaving and washing.

As he went through his toilette, which he did very carefully, and putting on now linen of dazzling whiteness, with which the most scrupulous person could have found no fault, his thoughts still ran upon the subject that had occupied his mind entirely for many days.

"There is danger in it, of course," he muttered to himself; "but I am used to danger; there was danger when Gonzalez provoked me, though it was not as great as that I stand in now. These English are stupid, but they are crafty also, and it may be that a trap will be set for me, perhaps is set already. Well, I will escape from it as I have from others. And, after all, I have one damning proof in my favour, one card that, if I am forced to play, must save me! What I have to do, shall be done to-day. I am resolved!"

His toilette was finished now, he was clean-shaved and well dressed from head to foot, and the Señor Miguel Guffanta stood in his room a very different-looking man from the one who had sat, an hour ago, smoking cigarettes in the hotel passage. Before he left it, he unlocked a portmanteau, and took from it a pocket-book into which he looked for a moment, and then he locked his door and descended the stairs.

"Going out for the day, Señor?" Diaz asked, as he peered out of his box.

"Yes. I am going to make a call on an English friend. *Adios*."

"*Adios*, Señor."

"It is as hot as Honduras," Señor Guffanta said to himself as he crossed to the shady side of the street. "I must walk slowly to keep myself cool."

He did walk slowly, making his way through Leicester Square and down Piccadilly, and, at nearly the bottom of the latter, turned off to the right and passed through several streets. Then, when he had arrived at a house which stood at a corner he stopped. He evidently had been here before, for he had found his way without any difficulty through the labyrinth of streets between this house and Leicester Square, and now he paused for one moment previous to mounting the doorstep. But, before he did so, he turned away and went a short distance down a side-street. The big house outside which he was standing formed the angle of two streets, and ran down the side one that the Señor had now turned into. At the back of it was a garden, fairly filled with trees, that ran some distance farther down this street, and into which an open-worked iron gate led, a gate through which any passerby could look. It was not a well-kept garden, and in it there was some undergrowth; and it was at this undergrowth, on the farthest right hand side, that Señor Guffanta peered for some few moments through the iron gate.

"It seems the same," he muttered to himself; "nothing appears disturbed since I was last here." Then he returned to the front of the house, and mounting the steps knocked at the hall door.

The footman who opened it had no time to ask the tall, well-dressed foreigner with the handsome face, who was standing before him, what he required, before the Señor said, in good English:

"Is Lord Penlyn within?"

"Yes, sir," the man answered. "Do you wish to see him?"

"Yes. Be good enough to take him my card, if you please," and he produced one bearing the name of *Señor Miguel Guffanta.* "Give him that," he said, "and say that I wish to see him."

The footman motioned him to a seat, and had put the card upon a salver to take to his master, when the Señor said "Stay, I will put a word upon it," and, taking a pencil from his pocket, he wrote underneath his name, "From Honduras."

"He will see me, I think," he said, "when he sees that."

The man bowed and went away, returning a few minutes afterwards to say that Lord Penlyn would see him, and the Señor followed him into the room in which so many other interviews had taken place.

Lord Penlyn rose and bowed, and Señor Guffanta returned the bow gravely, while he fixed his dark eyes intently on the other's face.

"You state on your card, Señor Guffanta, that you are from Honduras. I imagine, therefore, that you have come about a matter that at the present moment is of the utmost importance to me?" Lord Penlyn said.

"You refer to the late Mr. Cundall?" the Señor asked. "Yes, I do. Pray be seated."

"I knew him intimately," Señor Guffanta said. "It is about him and his murder that I have come to talk."

CHAPTER XIV.

Between the time when Lord Penlyn, Mr. Fordyce, and Stuart had consulted together as to the way in which some endeavours should be made to discover the murderer of Walter Cundall, and when the Señor Guffanta paid his visit to the former, a week had elapsed, a week in which a good many things had taken place.

The rewards offered both by the Government and by "the friends of the late Mr. Cundall," had been announced, and the magnitude of them, especially of the latter, had caused much excitement in the public mind, and had tended to keep the general interest in the tragedy alive. The Government reward of "five hundred pounds and a free pardon to some person, or persons, not the actual murderers," had been supplemented by another of one thousand pounds from the "friends and executors;" and the walls of every police-station were placarded with the notices. There was, moreover, attached to them a statement describing, as nearly as was possible from the meagre details known, the man who, in the garb of a labourer or mechanic, was last seen near the victim; and for his identification a reward was also offered.

But it was known in London, or, at least, very generally believed, that out of these rewards nothing whatever in the way of information had come; and, although the murder had not yet ceased to be a topic of conversation in all classes of society, it was generally spoken of as a case in which the murderer would never be brought to justice. Whoever had committed the crime had now had more than a week with which, either to escape from the neighbourhood or the country, or to entirely conceal his identity. It was not likely now, people said, that he would ever be found. And the world was also asking who were the friends, and, presumably, the heirs of the dead man, who were offering the large reward? To this question no one as yet had discovered the answer; all that was known, or told, being that two lawyers of standing, Mr. Bell, of Lincoln's Inn, and Mr. Fordyce, of Paper Buildings, were acting for these friends, and for Mr. Cundall's City representatives.

The detectives themselves, though they were careful not to say so, had really very little hope that they would ever succeed in tracing the assassin. Dobson (who, in spite of the stolidity of manner, and heaviness of appearance that had excited the contempt both of Señor Guffanta and of the landlord, Zarates, was not by any means lacking in shrewdness) plainly told Stuart, in one of their many interviews, that he did not think much would be done by finding the man called *Corot*, even if he were successful in doing so, which he very much doubted.

"You see, sir," he said, "it's this way. He evidently had some claim or other upon Mr. Cundall, or else it isn't likely that every time he wrote for money he would have got it, and that in good sums too. Then we've only seen the notes made by Mr. Cundall on the letters, saying that he sent this and that sum; but who's to know, when he sent them, if he didn't also send some friendly letter or other, acknowledging the justice of this man's demands? He evidently—I mean this *Corot*—did have some claim upon him; and supposing that he was —if we could find him—to prove that claim and show us the letters Mr. Cundall wrote him in return, where should we be then? The very fact of his being able to draw on him whenever he wanted money, would go a long way towards showing that he wouldn't be very likely to kill him."

"He threatens him in the last letter we have seen. Supposing that Mr. Cundall stopped the supplies after that, would not that probably excite his revengeful passions? These Spanish Americans do not stick at taking life when they fancy themselves injured."

"He evidently didn't stop them when he answered that letter, because he sent five hundred dollars. And it was written so soon before they both must have started—almost close together—from Honduras, that it wouldn't be likely any fresh demands would have been made," Dobson answered.

"They might have met in London, and quarrelled," Stuart replied; "and after the quarrel this *Corot* might have tracked him till he found a fitting opportunity, and then have killed him."

"Yes, he might," Dobson said, meditatively. "Anything *might* have happened."

"Only you don't think it likely?" the other asked.

"Well, frankly, Mr. Stuart, I don't. He had always got money out of him, and it wasn't likely the supplies would be stopped off altogether, so that to kill him would be killing the goose with the golden eggs."

"Who on earth could have killed him, then? Who would have had any reason to do so? You know everything connected with the case now, and with Mr. Cundall's life and strange, unknown, real position—do you suspect any one?"

"No," the detective said after a pause; "I can't say I do. Of course, at first, when I heard everything, the idea did strike me that Lord Penlyn, as the most interested person, might have done it."

"So it did me," Stuart said; "but after the interview Mr. Fordyce and I had with him the idea left my mind."

"Where does he say he was on the night of the murder—the night he was staying at that hotel?"

"He says he stayed at his club until twelve, and that then he walked about the streets till nearly two, thinking over the story his brother had told him, and then let himself into the hotel and went to bed."

"It is strange that he should have been about on that night alone. If he was going to be tried for the murder, it would tell badly against him; that is, unless he could prove that he was in the hotel before Mr. Cundall started to walk to Grosvenor Place from his club."

"He couldn't prove it, because all the servants were asleep; but, nevertheless, I am certain he did not do it."

"I don't think he did," Dobson replied, "and, at the same time, I can't believe *Corot* did it. But I wish I could find him, all the same."

"Do you think there is still a chance of your doing so?"

"There is always a chance," the other answered; "but I have exhausted nearly everything. You see, I have so little to go on, and I am obliged to say out openly, in every inquiry I make, that I am looking for a certain man of the name of *Corot*. And they all give me the same answer, that they never heard of such a name. Yet his name must have been *Corot*."

"I do not think so," Stuart said. "A Spaniard would sign an initial before his name just the same as an Englishman would, and no Englishman would sign himself simply 'Jones,' or 'Smith.'"

"It can't be a Christian name," Dobson said, "or they would have been sure to say so, and ask me 'What *Corot?*' or '*Corot* who' is it that you are looking for?"

"Lord Penlyn thinks it is a nickname," Stuart remarked.

"Then I shall certainly never find him. A man when he is travelling in a strange country doesn't use his nickname, and, as far as I can learn, there isn't any one here from the Republic of Honduras who ever heard of him; and it isn't any good asking people from British Honduras."

"Well," Stuart said, "we must go on trying by every means, and in the hopes that the amount of the rewards will lead to something. But there seems little prospect of our ever finding the cowardly assassin who slew him. Perhaps, after all, that labourer killed him for his watch and chain, and any money he might have about him. Such things have been done before."

"I don't believe that," Dobson said. "There was a motive for his murder. But, what was that motive?"

Then they parted, Stuart to have an interview with Lord Penlyn, and Dobson to again continue his investigations in similar resorts to the Hôtel Lepanto.

Meanwhile, Penlyn had nerved himself for another interview with Ida Raughton, an interview in which he was to tell her everything, and he went down to Belmont to do so.

He found her alone in her pretty drawing-room, Sir Paul having gone to Windsor on some business matter, and Miss Norris being out for a walk. She was still looking very pale, and her lover noticed that a paper was lying beside her in which was a column headed, "The murder of Mr. Cundall." Had she been reading that, he wondered, at the very time when he was on his way to tell her of the relationship that had existed between him and that other man who had loved her so dearly? When he had kissed her, wondering, as he did so, if it was the last kiss she would ever let him press upon her lips after she knew of what he had kept back from her at their last interview, she said to him:

"And now tell me what you have done towards finding Mr. Cundall's murderer? What steps have you taken, whom have you employed to search for that man?"

"It is thought," he answered, "that there is some man, now in England, who may have done it. A man whose name is *Corot*, and who was continually obtaining money from him."

"How is this known?"

"By some letters that have been found amongst Cundall's papers. Letters asking for money, and, in one case, threatening him if some was not sent at once; and with notes in his handwriting saying that different sums had been sent when demanded."

"*Corot*," she said, repeating the name to herself in a whisper, "*Corot*." Then, after a pause, she said, "No! That man is not the assassin."

"Not the assassin, Ida!" Penlyn said. "Why do you think he is not?"

"Because I have never known him, because the form of the man who slew him in my dream was familiar to me, and this man's form cannot be so."

"My darling," he said, "you place too much importance on this dream. Remember what fantasies of the brain they are, and how few of them have ever any bearing on the actual events of life."

"This was no fantasy," she answered, "no fantasy. When the murderer is discovered—if he ever is—it will be seen that I have known him. I am as sure of it as that I am sitting here. But who was he? Who was he? I have gone over and over again every man whom I have ever known, and yet I cannot bring to my mind which of all those men it is that that shrouded figure resembles." She paused again, and then she asked: "Has it been discovered yet whether he had any relations?"

"Yes, Ida," he said, rising from his seat and standing before her, while he knew that the time had come now when everything must be told. "Yes, he had one relation!"

"Who was he?" she asked, springing to her feet, while a strange lustre shone in her eyes. "Who was he? Tell me that."

"Oh, Ida," he said, "there is so much to tell! Will you hear me patiently while I tell you all?"

"Tell me everything," she replied. "I will listen."

Then he told her, standing there face to face with her. As he proceeded with his story, he could give no guess as to what effect it was having upon her, for she made no sign, but, from the seat into which she had sunk, gazed fixedly into his face. Once she shuddered slightly, and drew her dress nearer to her when he confessed that he had refused to part from him in peace; and, when she had read the letter that he had written on the night of his death, she wept silently for a few moments.

It had taken long in the telling, and the twilight of the summer night had come before he finished and she had learnt everything.

"That is what I came to tell you, Ida. Speak to me, and say that you forgive me for having kept it from your knowledge when last we met!"

"You said an hour ago," she replied, taking no heed of his prayer for forgiveness, "that dreams were idle fantasies of the brain. What if mine was such? What, if after all, I have seen the form of the man who murdered him, have spoken to him and let him kiss me, and have not recognised him?"

"Ida!" he said, "do you say this to me, to the man to whom you have plighted your love and faith? Do you mean that you suspect me of being my brother's murderer?"

"You did nothing," she answered, "to find out his murderer; you would have done nothing had that Will not been discovered."

"I obeyed his behest," he said, "and what I did was done also through my love of you."

Again she paused before she spoke, and then she said:

"It is time that you should go now, it is time that there should be no more love spoken of between us. But, if a time should ever come when it will be fitting for me to hear you speak of love to me once more—"

"Yes?"

"It will be when you can come to me and say that his murderer is brought

91

to justice."

"And until that time shall come, you cast me off?"

"If you take it in that light,—yes."

"I have sworn," he said, and she could not but notice the deep intensity of his voice, "upon his grave that my life shall be devoted to avenging him, and no power on earth shall stop me if I can but see my way to find the man who killed him. Even though I had still another brother, whom I had loved all my life, and he had done this deed, I would track him and bring him to punishment. I swear it before God—swear that I would not spare him! And my earnest and heartfelt prayer is that the day may arrive when, as you and I desire, I may be able to come and tell you that he is brought to justice."

"Ah! yes."

"Only," he continued, still with a deep solemnity of voice that went to her heart, "when I do so come I shall come to tell you that alone—there will be with that news no pleadings of love upon my tongue. You have doubted, but just now, whether you have not seen my brother's murderer standing before you, whether the kiss of Cain has not been upon your lips. You have reproached me for my silence, you have cast me off, unless I can prove myself not an assassin. Well, so be it! By the blessing of heaven, I will prove it—but for the love which you have withdrawn from me I will ask no more. You say it is to be mine again conditionally. I will not take it back, either with or without conditions. It is restored to you; it would be best that henceforth you should keep it."

Then, with but the slightest inclination of his head, he left her, and went out from the house. And Ida, after once endeavouring to make her lips utter the name of Gervase, fell prostrate on the couch.

"He will never come back to me," she wailed; "he will never come back. I have thrown his love away for ever. God forgive and pity me."

CHAPTER XV.

"I knew him intimately," Señor Guffanta said, "it is about him and his murder that I have come to talk."

These were the words with which he had responded to Lord Penlyn's reception of him; and, as he uttered them, a hope had sprung up into the young man's breast that, in the handsome Spaniard who stood before him, some one might have been found who, from his knowledge of his brother, would be able to throw some light upon, or clue to, his death.

"I cannot tell you," he said, "how welcome this information is to me. We have tried everything in our power to gather some knowledge that might lead towards finding—first, some one who would be likely to have a reason for his death; and, afterwards, the man who killed him. If you knew him intimately, it may be that you can assist us."

The Señor had taken the seat offered him by Penlyn, and from the time that he had first sat down, until now, he had not removed his dark piercing eyes from the other's face. But, as he continued to fix his glance upon Penlyn, there had come into his own face a look of surprise, a look that seemed to express a baffled feeling of consternation.

"*Caramba*," he said to himself while the other was speaking. "*Caramba*, what mystery is there here? I have made a mistake. I have erred in some way; how have I deceived myself? Yet I could have sworn by the blood of San Pedro that I was sure."

Then, when Lord Penlyn had ceased speaking, he said aloud:

"You will pardon me—but I am labouring under no mistake? You are Lord Penlyn?"

The other looked at him for a moment, wondering what such a question meant. Then he answered him:

"There is no mistake. I am Lord Penlyn."

The Spaniard passed his hand across his eyes as he heard this, but did not speak; and Lord Penlyn said:

"May I ask why you inquire?"

"Because—because I had thought—because I wished to be sure of whom I was speaking with."

"You may rest assured. And now, sir, let me ask you what you know about this unhappy Mr. Cundall and his life?"

"I know much about him. To begin with, I know that he was your brother—your elder brother—and that you have come to possess his fortune."

Lord Penlyn started and said: "You know that? May I ask how you know it?"

"It is not necessary for me to say. It is sufficient that I do know it. But it is not of that that I have come to talk."

"Of what have you come to talk then?"

"Of his murderer."

"Of his murderer!" the other repeated. "Oh! Señor Guffanta, is it possible that you can have any clue, is it possible that you think you will be able to find the man who killed him?"

"*I am sure of it.*"

Lord Penlyn stared at him as he spoke, stared at him while in his mind there was a feeling of astonishment, mixed with something like awe, of his strange visitor. This dark, powerful-looking stranger, sat there before him perfectly calm and unmoved, looking straight at him as he spoke these words of import, "I am sure of it," and spoke them as though he was speaking of some ordinary incident. And in his calmness there was something that told the other that it was born of certainty.

"If you can do that, Señor Guffanta," he said, "there is nothing that you can ask from me, there is nothing that I can give that—"

"There is nothing I want of you," the Spaniard said, interrupting him, and making a disdainful motion with his long, brown hand. "I am not a paid police spy."

"I beg your pardon," the other answered. "I had no thought of offence. Only, sir, it is the wish of my life, and of some others who knew and loved him, to see him avenged.

"And it is the wish of my life also. Will you hear a short story?"

"I will hear anything you have to say."

"Then listen. I was born in Honduras, the child of a Spanish lady and of a friend of the old Englishman, Cundall, him from whom your brother's wealth was derived. That friend was a scoundrel, a man who tricked my mother into a marriage with him under a false name, who never was her husband at all. When they had been married, as she thought, for some few years, and when another child, my sister, had been born, she found out the deception, and—she killed him."

"Killed him!" Penlyn exclaimed.

"Yes, dead! We Spaniards brook no dishonour, we never allow a wrong to pass unavenged. She showed him the evidence of his falsehood in one hand, and with the other she shot him dead upon his own verandah. She was tried and instantly acquitted, and, in consideration of the wrong she had suffered, a law was made constituting her legally his wife, and making us children legitimate. But the disgrace was to her—a high-minded, noble woman—too much; she fell ill and died. Then the old man, Cundall, seeing that it was his friend's evil-doing that had led to our being orphans, said that henceforth we should be his care. So we grew up, and I had learnt to look upon myself and my sister as his heirs, when one day there came another who, it was easy to see, had supplanted us. It was the English lad, Walter Cundall."

"I begin to see," Penlyn said.

"At first," Señor Guffanta went on, "I hated him for spoiling our chances, but at last I could hate him no longer. Gradually, his gentle disposition, his way of interceding for me with his uncle, when I had erred, above all his tenderness to my poor sister, who was sick and deformed, won my love. Had he been my brother I could not have loved him more. Then—then, as years went on, I committed a fault, and the old man cast me off for ever. Another man tried to take from me the woman I loved—she was a vile thing worth no man's love; but—no matter how—I avenged myself. But from that day the old man turned against me, and would neither see nor hear of me again.

"A year or two passed and then I heard from Walter, for my sister and I had left Los Torros (the town where we had all lived) and had gone elsewhere, that the old man was dead. 'He has left everything to me,' Walter wrote, 'and there is no mention of you nor Juanna, but be assured neither of you shall ever want for anything.'"

"Stop," Lord Penlyn said, "you need tell me no more. I know the rest."

"You know the rest?" Señor Guffanta said, looking fixedly at him, "You know the rest?"

"Yes. You are *Corot*."

A bewildered look came over the Spaniard's face, and then, after a second's pause, he said:

"Yes. I am *Corot*. It was the name given me by the Mestizos amongst whom I played as a boy, and it kept to me. It is you, then, Lord Penlyn, who has set this Dobson to look for me?"

"Yes; we found your letters to him, and from one of them we believed you to be in England. We thought that—that—"

"That I killed him?"

"You threatened him in one of your letters. We were justified in thinking so."

"He, at least, did not think so. Read this."

He took from his pocket a letter written by Walter Cundall during the few days he had been back in England, and gave it to Penlyn. It ran:

"*June*, 188—.

"MY DEAR COROT,

"I am delighted to hear you are in England, and have got an appointment as agent for Don Rodriguez in London. Perhaps, now, I shall have some respite from those fearful threats which, at intervals, from your boyhood, you have hurled at me, at Juanna, and every one you really love. Come and see me when you can, only come as late as possible as I am out much; and we will have a talk about the old place and old times.

"Ever yours, in haste, W. C.

"P.S.—I wish poor Juanna could have lived to know of your good fortune."

"Do you think I should murder that man, Lord Penlyn?" Señor Guffanta asked quietly. "That man who, when he heard of my good fortune, could think of how happy it would have made my beloved sister—she who is now in her grave."

"Whatever I may have thought must be ascribed to the intense desire I and my friends have to find his murderer, and you must pardon the suspicion that came to our minds in reading your letters. But, Señor Guffanta, let us forget that and speak about finding him, since you also are anxious to avenge Walter, and feel sure that you can do so."

"I am perfectly sure. And before long I shall stand face to face with him. Then his doom is certain!"

Again Lord Penlyn noticed the self-constrained calm of the man, and again he told himself that he spoke with such an air of certainty that it was impossible to doubt him. For one moment the thought came to his mind that this apparent calmness, this certainty of finding the murderer, might be a rôle assumed by Guffanta to prevent suspicion falling upon him. But on reflection that thought took flight. Had he been the murderer he would never have revealed himself, would never have allowed it to be known that he was *Corot*, the man against whom circumstances had looked so black. And Cundall's letter was sufficient to show that what the Señor had told him, about the friendship that had existed between them, was true.

"You must know more than any of us, Señor Guffanta, as no doubt you do —to inspire you with such confidence of finding him. Had he any enemy in Honduras, who may now be in England, and have done this deed?"

"To my knowledge, none. He was a man who made friends, not enemies."

"How then, do you hope to find the man who killed him?"

"I hope nothing, Lord Penlyn, for I am sure to find him. What will you say when I tell you that I have seen his murderer's face?"

"You have seen his face? You know it!" the other exclaimed, springing to his feet. "Oh, let me at once send for the detectives and the lawyers, so that you may describe him to them, and let them endeavour to find him. But," he said suddenly, "where have you seen him?"

There was an almost contemptuous smile upon the Señor Guffanta's face as he said:

"Send for no one—at least, not yet. If by the detectives you mean Dobson, the heavy man, he will not assist me, and of the lawyers I know nothing; and at present I will not tell you when and where I have seen this man. But, sir— but, Lord Penlyn, I know one thing. When that man and I once more stand face to face, Walter Cundall, who shielded me from his uncle's wrath, who was as a brother to my beloved Juanna, will be avenged."

"What will you do?" Penlyn asked in an almost awestruck whisper. "You will not take the law into your own hands and kill him?"

"No; it maybe not! But with these hands alone," and he held them out extended to Penlyn as he spoke, "I will drag him to a prison which he shall only leave for a scaffold. Drag him there, I say, unless my blood gets the better of my reason, and I throttle him like a dog by the way."

He, too, had risen in his excitement; and as he stood towering in his height, which was great, above the other, and extended his long sinewy hands in front of him, while his deep brown skin turned to an almost darker hue, Penlyn felt that this man before him would be the avenger of his brother's death. So terrible did he look, that the other wondered how that murderer would feel when he should be in his grasp.

He stepped forward to Guffanta and held out his hand to him. "Sir," he said, "I thank God that you and I have met. But can we do nothing to assist you in your search? May I not tell the detectives what you know?"

"You may tell them everything I have told you; it will not enable them to be in my way. But what I have to do I must do by myself." He paused a moment; then he said: "It may be that when you do tell them, they will still think that I am the man—"

"No, no!"

"Yes, it may be so. Well, if they want to spy upon my actions, if they want to know what I do and where I go, I am to be found at the Hôtel Lepanto— that is when I am not here in this house, for I must ask you—I have a reason —to let me come to you as I want."

Penlyn bowed, and said some words to the effect that he should always be free of the house, and the other continued:

"My business here as agent for Don Rodriguez, a wealthy merchant of Honduras, will not occupy me much at present, the rest of my time will be devoted to the one purpose of finding that man."

"I pray that you may be successful."

"I shall be successful," the Spaniard answered quietly. "And now," he said, "I will ask you to do one thing."

"Ask me anything and I will do it."

"You have a garden behind your house," Señor Guffanta said, "how is admission obtained to it?"

Lord Penlyn stared at him wonderingly, not knowing what this question might mean, and then he said:

"There is an entrance from the back of this house, and another from an iron gate in the side street. But why do you ask? no one ever goes into it. It is damp, and even the paths are partly overgrown with weeds."

"There are keys to those entrances?"

"Yes."

"And in your possession?" and, as he spoke, his dark eyes were fixed very intently on the young man.

"They are somewhere about the house, but they are never used."

"I wish them found. Then, when they are found, I must ask you to give me your word of honour that no living creature, not even you yourself, will enter that garden without my knowing it. Will you do this?"

"I will do it," Penlyn said. "But I wish you would tell me your reason."

"I will tell you nothing more at present. But remember that I have a task to perform and that I shall do it."

Then he left him, and walked away to the neighbourhood of Leicester Square.

"What I have seen to-day," he said to himself, "would have baffled many a man. But you, Miguel, are different from other men. You are not baffled, you are only still more determined to do what you have to do. But who is he?—who is he? *Caramba!* he is not Lord Penlyn!"

<h1 style="text-align:center">CHAPTER XVI.</h1>

"The story about this Spaniard, Guffanta, is a strange one," Philip Smerdon wrote from Occleve Chase to Lord Penlyn, who had informed him of the visit he had received and the revelations made by the Señor, "but I may as well tell you at once that I don't believe it, although you say that the lawyers, as well as Stuart and Dobson, are inclined to do so. My own opinion is that, though he may not have killed Mr. Cundall, he is still telling you a lie—for some reason of his own, as to the friendship that existed between them; and he probably thinks that by pretending to be able to find the man, he will get some money from you. With regard to his having been face to face with the murderer, why, if so, does he not say on what occasion and when? To know his face *as that of the murderer*, is to say, what in plainer words would be, that he had either known he was about to commit the act, or that he had witnessed it. It admits of no other interpretation, and, consequently, what becomes of his avowed love for Cundall, if he knew of the contemplated deed and did not prevent it, or, having witnessed it, did not at once arrest or kill his aggressor? You may depend upon it, my dear Gervase, that this man's talk is nothing but empty braggadocio, with, as I said before, the probable object of extracting money from you as he previously extracted it from your brother.

"As to the locking up of the garden and allowing no one to enter it, I am inclined to think that it is simply done with the object of making a pretence of mysteriously knowing something that no one else knows. And it is almost silly, for your garden would scarcely happen to be selected by the murderer as a place to visit, and what object could he have in so visiting it? However, as it is a place never used, I should gratify him in this case, only I would go a little farther than he wishes, and never allow it to be opened—not even when he desires it."

The letter went on to state that Smerdon was still very busy over the summer accounts at Occleve Chase, and should remain there some time; he might, however, he added, shortly run up to town for a night.

A feeling of disappointment came over Penlyn as he read this letter from his friend. During the two or three days that had elapsed between writing to Smerdon and receiving his answer, he had been buoyed up with the hope that in Guffanta the man had been discovered who would be the means of bringing the assassin to justice, and this hope had been shared by all the other men interested in the same cause. But he had come, in the course of his long friendship with Philip Smerdon, to place such utter reliance upon his judgment, and to accept so thoroughly his ideas, that the very fact of his doubting the Señor's statement, and looking upon it as a mere vulgar attempt to extort money from him, almost led him also to doubt whether, after all, he had not too readily believed the Spaniard.

Yet, he reflected, his actions, as he stood before him foretelling the certain doom of that assassin when once they should again be face to face, and his calm certainty that such would undoubtedly happen, bore upon them the impress of truth. And his story had earned the belief of the others—that, surely, was in favour of it being true. Stuart had seen him, had listened to what he had to say, and had formed the opinion that he was neither lying nor acting. Dobson also, the man who to the Señor's mind was ridiculous and incapable, had been told everything, and he, too, had come to the conclusion that Guffanta's story was an honest one, and that, of all other men, he who in some mysterious manner, knew the murderer's face, would be the most likely to eventually bring him to justice. Only, he thought that the Señor should be made to divulge where and when he had so seen his face; that would give him and his brethren a clue, he said, which might enable them to assist him in tracking the man. And he was also very anxious to know what the secret was that led to his desiring Lord Penlyn to have the garden securely closed and locked. He could find in his own mind no connecting link between the place of death in the Park and Lord Penlyn's garden (although he remembered that, strangely enough, his lordship was the dead man's brother), and he was desirous that the Señor should confide in him. But the latter would tell him nothing more than he had already made known, and Dobson, who had always in his mind's eye the vision of the large rewards that would come to the man who found the murderer, was forced to be content and to work, as he termed it, "in the dark."

"You must wait, my good Dobson, you must wait," the Spaniard said, "until I tell you that I want your assistance, though I do not think it probable that I shall ever want it. You could not find out that I was *Corot*, you know, although I had many times the pleasure of lunching at the next table to you; I do not think that you will be able any the better to find the man I seek. But when I find him, Dobson, I promise you that you shall have the pleasure of arresting him, so that the reward shall come to you. That is, if I do not have to arrest him suddenly upon the moment, myself, so as to prevent him escaping."

"And what are you doing now, *Signor?*" Dobson asked, giving him a title more familiar to him in its pronunciation than the Spanish one, "what are you doing to find him?"

"I am practising a virtue, my friend, that I have practised much in my life. I am waiting."

"I don't see that waiting is much good, Signor. There is not much good ever done by waiting."

"The greatest good in the world, Dobson, the very greatest. And you do not see now, Dobson, because you do not know what I know. So you, too, must be virtuous, and wait."

It was only with banter of a slightly concealed nature such as this that Señor Guffanta would answer Dobson, but, light as his answers were, he had still managed to impress the detective with the idea that, sooner or later, he would achieve the task he had vowed to perform. "But," as the man said to one of his brethren, "why don't he get to work, why don't he do something? He won't find the man in that Hôtel Lepanto where he sits smoking cigarettes half the day, nor yet in Lord Penlyn's house where he goes every night."

"Perhaps he thinks his lordship did it, after all," the other answered, "and is watching *him*."

"No," Dobson said, "he don't think that. But I can't make out who the deuce he does suspect."

It was true enough that Guffanta did pass a considerable time in the Hôtel Lepanto, smoking cigarettes, and always thinking deeply, whether seated in the corridor or in his own room upstairs. But, although he had not allowed himself to say one word to any of the other men on the subject, and still spoke with certainty of ere long finding the murderer, he was forced to acknowledge that, for the time, he was baffled. And then, as he did acknowledge this, he would rise from his chair and stretch out his long arms, and laugh grimly to himself. "But only for a time, Miguel," he would say, "only for a time. He will come to you at last, he will come to you as the bird comes to the net. Wait, wait, wait! You may meet him to-day, to-night! *Por Dios*, you will surely trap him at last!"

Meanwhile Lord Penlyn, when he was left alone, and when he could distract his thoughts from the desire of his life, the finding of the man who had slain Walter Cundall, was very unhappy. Those thoughts would then turn to the girl he had loved deeply, to the girl whom he had cast off because she had ventured to let the idea come into her mind that it was he who might have done the deed. He had cast her off in a moment when there had come into his heart a revulsion of feeling towards her, a feeling of horror that she, of all others in the world, could for one moment harbour such an idea against him. Yet, he admitted to himself, there were grounds upon which even the most, loving of women might be excused for having had such thoughts. He had misled her at first, he had kept back the truth from her, he had given her reasons for suspicion—even against him, her lover. And now they were parted, he had renounced her, and yet he knew that he loved her as fondly as ever; she was the one woman in the world to him. Would they ever come together again? Was it possible, that if he, who had told her that never more in this world would he speak to her of love, should go back again and kneel at her feet and plead for pardon, it would be granted to him? If he could think that; if he could think that when once his brother was avenged he might so plead and be so forgiven, then he could take courage and look forward hopefully to the future. But at present they were strangers, they were as much parted as though they had never met; and he was utterly unhappy.

When Guffanta had declared himself; it had been in his mind to write and tell her all that he had newly learnt; but he could not bring himself to write an ordinary letter to her. It might be that, notwithstanding the deep interest she took in his unhappy brother's fate, she would refuse to open any letter in his handwriting, and would regard it almost as an insult. Yet he wanted to let her know what had now transpired, and he at last decided what to do. He asked Stuart to direct an envelope for him to her, and he put a slip of paper inside it, on which he wrote:

"*Corot* has disclosed himself, and he, undoubtedly, is not the murderer. He, however, has some strange knowledge of the actual man in his possession which he will not reveal, but says that he is certain, at last, to bring him to justice."

That was all, and he put no initials to it, but he thought that the knowledge might be welcome to her.

He had not expected any answer to this letter, or note, and from Ida none came, but a day or two after he had sent it, he received a visit from Sir Paul Raughton. The baronet had come up to town especially to see him, and having learnt from the footman that Lord Penlyn was at home, he bade the man show him to his master, and followed him at once. As Penlyn rose to greet him, he noticed that Sir Paul's usually good-humoured face bore a very serious expression, and he knew at once that the interview they were about to have would be an important one.

"I have come up to London expressly to see you, Lord Penlyn," Sir Paul said, shaking hands with him coldly, "because I wish to have a thorough explanation of the manner in which you see fit to conduct yourself towards my daughter. No," he said, putting up his hand, as he saw that Penlyn was about to interrupt him, "hear me for one moment. I may as well tell you at once that Ida, that my daughter, has told me everything that you have confided to her with regard to your relationship to Mr. Cundall—which, I think, it was your duty also to have told me—and she has also told me the particulars of your last interview with her."

"I parted with her in anger," the other answered, "because there seemed to have come into her mind some idea that I—that I might have slain my brother."

"And for that, for a momentary suspicion on her part, a suspicion that would scarcely have entered her head had her mind not been in the state it is, you have seen fit to cast her off, and to cancel your engagement!"

"It was she, Sir Paul, who bade me speak no more of love to her," Penlyn said, "she who told me that, until I had found the murderer of my brother, I was to be no more to her."

"And she did well to tell you so," Sir Paul said; "for to whom but to you, his brother and his heir, should the task fall of avenging his cruel murder?"

"That, I told her, I had sworn to do, and yet she suspected me. And, Sir Paul, God knows I did not mean the words of anger that I spoke; I have bitterly repented of them ever since. If Ida will let me recall them, if she will give me again her love—if you think there is any hope of that—I will go back and sue to her for it on my knees."

The baronet looked thoughtfully at him for a moment, and then he said. "Do you know that she is very ill?"

"Ill! Why have I not been told of it?"

"Why should you have been told? It was your words to her, and her excitement over your brother's murder, that has brought her illness about."

"Let me go and see her?"

"You cannot see her. She is in bed and delirious from brain fever; and on her lips there are but two names which she repeats incessantly, your own and your brother's."

The young man leant forward on the table and buried his head in his hands, as he said: "Poor Ida! poor Ida! Why should this trouble also come to you? And why need I have added to your unhappiness by my cruelty?" Then he looked up and said to Sir Paul: "When will she be well enough for me to go to her and plead for pardon? Will it be soon, do you think?"

"I do not know," the other answered sadly. "But if, when the delirium has left her, I can tell her that you love her still and regret your words, it may go far towards her recovery."

"Tell her that," Penlyn said, "and that my love is as deep and true as ever, and that, at the first moment she is in a fit condition to hear it, I will, myself, come and tell her so with my own lips. And also tell her that, never again, will I by word or deed cause her one moment's pain."

"I am glad to hear you speak like this," Sir Paul said, "glad to find that I had not allowed my darling to give herself to a man who would cast her off because she, for one moment, harboured an unworthy suspicion of him."

"This unhappy misunderstanding has been the one blot upon our love," Penlyn said; "if I can help it, there shall never be another."

As he spoke these words, Sir Paul put his hand kindly on his shoulder, and Penlyn knew that, in him, he had one who would faithfully carry his message of love to the woman who was the hope of his life.

"And now," Sir Paul said, "I want you to give me full particulars of everything that has occurred since that miserable night. I want to know everything fully, and from your lips. What Ida has been able to tell me has been sadly incoherent."

Then, once more—as he had had now so often to go over the sad history to others, with but little fresh information added to each recital—Lord Penlyn told Sir Paul everything that he knew, and of the strange manner in which the Señor Guffanta had come into the matter, as well as his apparent certainty of eventually finding the murderer.

"You do not think it is a bold ruse to throw off suspicion from himself?" Sir Paul asked. "A daring man, such as he seems to be, might adopt such a plan."

"No," the other answered, "I do not. There is something about the man, stranger as he is, that not only makes me feel certain that he is perfectly truthful in what he says, and that he really does possess some strange knowledge of the assassin that will enable him to find that man at last, but also makes the others feel equally certain."

"They all believe in him, you say?" Sir Paul asked thoughtfully.

"All! That is, all but Philip Smerdon, who is the only one who has not seen him. And I am sure that, if he too saw him and heard him, he would believe."

"Philip Smerdon is a thorough man of the world," Sir Paul said, "I should be inclined to give weight to his judgment."

"I am sure that he is wrong in this case, and that when he sees Guffanta, he will acknowledge himself to be so. No one who has seen him can doubt his earnestness."

"What can be the mystery concerning your garden? A mystery that is a double one, because it brings your house, of all houses in London, into connection with the murder of the very man who, at the moment, was the actual owner of it? That is inexplicable!"

"It is," Penlyn said, "inexplicable to every one. But the Señor tells us that when we know what he knows, and when he has brought the murderer to bay, we shall see that it is no mystery at all."

CHAPTER XVII.

Although the Señor Guffanta had not, as yet, in answer to many questions put to him, been able to say positively that he was on the immediate track of the murderer of Walter Cundall, he still continued to inspire confidence in those by whom he was surrounded; and it had now come to be quite accepted amongst all whom he met at Occleve House that, although he was working darkly and mysteriously, he was in some way nearing the object he had in view. It may have been his intense self-confidence, the outward appearance of which he never allowed to fail, that impressed them thus, or the stern look with which he accompanied any words he ever uttered in connection with the assassin; or it may have been the manner he had of making inquiries of all descriptions of every one who had known anything of the dead man, that led them to believe in him; but that they did believe in him there was no doubt.

In the time he had at his disposal, after transacting any affairs he might have to manage for the merchant who had appointed him his agent in London, he was continually passing from one spot to another, sometimes spending hours at Mr. Cundall's house in Grosvenor Place, and sometimes a long period of time each day at Occleve House; but to no one did he ever say one word indicative of either success or failure. And, when he was alone in either of these places, his proceedings were of a nature that, had they been witnessed by any one, would have caused them to wonder what it was that he was seeking for. He would study attentively every picture that was a portrait, whether painting or engraving, and for photograph albums, of which there were a number in both houses, he seemed to have an untiring curiosity. He would look them over and over again, pausing occasionally a long time over some man's face that struck him, and then would turn the leaf and go on to another; and then, when he had, for the second or third time exhausted one album, he would take up another, and again go through that.

To Dobson, who was by the outside world regarded as the man who had the whole charge of the case, the Señor's actions, and his absolute refusal to confide in him, were almost maddening. To any question that he asked, he received nothing but the regular answer, "Patience, my good Dobson, patience," and with that he was obliged to be content. For himself, he had done nothing; he was no nearer having any idea now as to who the murderer was than he had been the morning after the deed had been committed, and as day after day went by, he began to doubt whether Guffanta was any nearer finding the man who was wanted than he was.

"But if he doesn't do something pretty quick," he said to one of the men who was supposed to be employed under him in investigating the case, "I shall put a spoke in his wheel."

"Why, what will you do, Mr. Dobson?" his underling asked.

"I shall just go up to the Home Office, and when they ask me, as they do regular, if I have got anything to report in connection with the Cundall case, I shall tell them that the Señor professes to know a good deal that he won't divulge, and ask them to have him up before them, and make him tell what he do know."

"And suppose he won't tell, Mr. Dobson? What then?"

"Why, he'll be made to tell, that's all! It isn't right, and it isn't fair that, if he knows anything and can't find the man himself, he should be allowed to keep it a secret and prevent me from earning the reward. I'll bet I'd soon find the man if I had his information—that is, if he's really got any."

"Don't it strike you, Mr. Dobson," the other asked, "that there is some mystery in connection with Occleve House that he knows of? What with his having the garden locked up, and his always being about there!"

"It did once, but I have thought it over, and I can't see how the house can be connected with it. You see, on that night it so happened there was no one in the house but the footmen and the women servants. His lordship and the valet had gone off to stay at the hotel, and Mr. Smerdon had gone down in the morning to the country seat, so what could the murderer have had to do with that particular house? And it ain't the house the Señor seems to think so much about—it's the garden."

"I can't make that garden business out at all," the other said; "what on earth has the garden got to do with it?"

"That's just what he won't say. But you mark my words, I ain't going to stand it much longer, and he'll have to say. If he don't tell pretty soon what he knows, I shall get the Home Office to make him."

Meanwhile the Señor, who had bewildered Lord Penlyn and Mr. Stuart by the connection which he seemed to feel certain existed between the garden of Occleve House and the murder in the Park, excited their curiosity still more when he suddenly announced one evening that he was going down, with his lordship's permission, to pay a visit to Occleve Chase.

"Certainly," Penlyn replied, "you have my full permission; I shall be glad if you will always avail yourself of anything that is mine. But, Señor Guffanta, you connect my houses strangely with this search you are making— first it was this one, and now it is Occleve Chase—; do you not think you should confide a little more in me?"

"I cannot confide in you yet, Lord Penlyn. And, frankly, I do not know that I have much to confide. Nor am I connecting Occleve Chase with the murder. But I have a wish to see that house. I am fond of old houses, and it was Walter's property once though he never possessed it. I might draw inspiration from a visit to it."

For the first time since he had known the Señor, Lord Penlyn doubted if he was speaking frankly to him. It was useless for Guffanta to pretend that he was not now connecting Occleve Chase in his own mind with the murder, as he had certainly connected the old disused garden previously—but whom did he suspect? For one moment the idea flashed through his mind that perhaps, after all, he still suspected him; but another instant's thought served to banish that idea. Whatever this dark, mysterious man might be working out in his own brain, at least it could not be that. Had he not said that, by some strange chance, he had once stood face to face with the assassin? Having done so, there could be no thought in his mind that he, Penlyn, was that assassin. But, if it was not him whom he suspected, who was it?

"Well," he said, "you must take your own way, Señor Guffanta, and I can only hope it may land you aright. Only, if you would confide more in me, I should be glad."

"I tell you that at present I cannot do so. Later on, perhaps, you will understand my reason for silence. Meanwhile, be sure that before long this man will be in my power."

Then the Señor asked for some directions as to the manner of reaching Occleve Chase, and Lord Penlyn told him the way to travel there.

"And I will give you a letter to my friend, Philip Smerdon, who is down there just now," he said, "and he will make your stay comfortable. He, of course, has also a great interest in the affair we all have so much at heart, and you will be able to talk it over with him; though, I must tell you, that he has very little hopes of your ultimate success."

"Ah! he has no hopes. Well, we shall see! I myself have the greatest of hopes. And this Mr. Smerdon, this friend of yours, I have never yet seen him. I shall be glad to know him."

So when the letter of introduction was written, the Señor departed, and on the next day he started for Occleve Chase.

He travelled down from London comfortably ensconced in a first-class smoking compartment, from which he did not move until the train deposited him at the nearest station to Occleve Chase. The few fellow-passengers who got in and out on the way, looked curiously at the dark, sunburnt man, who sat back in the corner, twisting up strange-looking little cigarettes, and gazing up at the roof or at the country they were passing through; but of none of them did the Señor take any notice, beyond giving one swift glance at each as they entered. It had become a habit of this man's life now to give such a glance at every one with whom he came into contact. Perhaps he thought that if he missed one face, he might miss that of the man for whom he was seeking.

At the station nearest to the "Chase" he alighted, and taking his small bag in his hand, walked over to the public-house opposite, and asked if a cab could be provided to take him the remainder of his journey, which he knew to be about four miles.

"I beg your pardon, sir," a neat-looking groom said, rising from a table at which he had been sitting drinking some beer, and touching his hat respectfully, "but might I ask if you're going over there on any business?"

"Who are you?" Señor Guffanta asked, looking at him.

"Beg pardon, sir, but I'm one of Lord Penlyn's grooms, and I thought if you were going over on any business you might like me to drive you over. I have the dog-cart here."

"I am a friend of Lord Penlyn's," the Señor answered, "and I am going to stay at Occleve Chase for a day or so. I have brought a letter of introduction to Mr. Smerdon."

"That's a pity, sir," the man said, "because Mr. Smerdon has gone up to London by the fast train. I have just driven him over from the Chase."

"He is gone to London?" the Señor said quietly. "And when will he be back, do you think?"

"He did not say, sir."

"Very well. If you will drive me there now, I shall be obliged to you."

The groom put the horse to, and fetched the dog-cart round from the stable, wondering as he did so who the quiet, dark gentleman was who was going to stay all alone at the "Chase" for a day or so; and then having put the Señor's bag in, he asked him to get up, and they started for OccleveChase.

On the road Señor Guffanta made scarcely any remark, speaking only once of the prettiness of the country they were passing through, and once of the action of the horse, which seemed to excite his admiration; and then he was silent till they reached the house, a fine old Queen Anne mansion in excellent preservation. He introduced himself to the housekeeper who came forward in the hall, and said:

"I have a letter of introduction to Mr. Smerdon; I had hoped to find him here. Perhaps it would be well if I gave it to you instead."

"As you please, sir, but it is not necessary. Lord Penlyn's friends often come here, when they are in this part of the country, to see the house. It is considered worth going over. If you please, sir, I will send a servant up with your bag."

"I thank you," the Señor said, with his usual grave courtesy, "but I shall not trouble you much. I dare say by to-morrow I shall have seen all I want to."

"As you please, sir."

He followed the neat-looking housemaid to the room he was to occupy, after having told the housekeeper that the simplest meal in the evening would be sufficient for him, and then, when he had made some slight toilette, he descended to the lower rooms of the house. The old servant again came forward and volunteered her services to show him the curiosities and antiquities of the place; but Señor Guffanta politely told her that he would not trouble her.

"I am fond of looking at pictures," he said, "I will inspect those if you please. But I am acquainted with the styles of different masters, so I do not require a guide. If you will tell me where the pictures are in this house, I shall be obliged to you."

"They are everywhere, sir," she answered. "In the picture-gallery, the dining-room, hall, and library."

"I will go through the library first, if you please. Which is that?"

The servant led the way to a large, lofty room, with windows looking out upon a well-kept lawn, and told him that this was the room.

"These pictures will not take you long, sir," she said, "it's mostly books that are here. And Mr. Smerdon generally spends most of his time here at his accounts; sometimes he passes whole days at that desk."

She seemed inclined to be garrulous, and Señor Guffanta, who wished to be alone, took, at random, a book from one of the shelves, and throwing himself into a chair, began to read it. Then, saying that she would leave him—perhaps taking what he intended as a hint—she withdrew.

When he was left alone he took no notice of the pictures on the walls (they were all paintings of long-past days), but, rising, went over to the desk where she had said that Mr. Smerdon spent hours. There were a few papers lying about on it which he turned over, and he pulled at the drawers to see if they would open, but they were all locked fast.

"This room is no good to me," he said to himself, "I must try others."

Gradually, as the day wore on, the Señor went from apartment to apartment in the house, inspecting each one carefully. In the drawing-room he spent a great deal of time, for here he had found what, both at Occleve House and at Mr. Cundall's house in Grosvenor Place, had interested him more than anything else—some photograph albums. These he turned over very carefully, as he had done with the others in London, and then he closed them and went to another room.

"Did he ever know," he muttered once, "that the day would come when I should be looking eagerly for his portrait—did he know that, and did some instinct prompt him never to have a record made of his craven face? And yet, he shall not escape me! Yet, I will find him!"

Later in the evening, when he had eaten sparingly of the dinner that had been prepared for him, and had drunk still more sparingly of the choice wine set before him, confining himself almost entirely to water, he sent for the housekeeper and said:

"I think I have seen everything of importance here in the way of art, and Lord Penlyn is to be congratulated on his treasures. Some of the pictures are very valuable."

"They are thought to be so, sir," the woman answered. In her own mind, and after a conversation with another of the head servants, she had put Señor Guffanta down as some foreign picture-dealer, or *connoisseur*, who had received permission from her master to inspect the collection at the "Chase," and, consequently, she considered him entitled to give an opinion, especially as that opinion was a favourable one. "They are thought to be so, sir."

"Yes; no doubt. But I have seen them all now, and I will leave to-morrow."

"Very well, sir."

"So, if you please, I will have that young man to drive me to the station. I will go by the train that he told me Mr. Smerdon travelled by."

That night, as Señor Guffanta paced up and down the avenue leading to the house and smoked his cigarettes, or as he tossed upon his bed, he confessed that he was no nearer to his task.

"Everything fails me," he said; "and yet, a week ago, I would have sworn by San Pedro that I should have caught him by now. There is only one chance —one hope left. If that fails me too, then I must lose all courage. Will it fail me?—will it fail?"

"It is strange, too," he said once to himself in the night, when, having been unable to sleep, he had risen and thrown his window open and was gazing from it, "that I cannot meet this man Smerdon, this man who believes that I shall fail—as, *por Dios!* I almost now myself believe! Strange, also, that he should have left on the very day I came here. I should like to see him. It may be that I shall do so in London to-morrow."

He left Occleve Chase at the time fixed, and by his liberality to the housekeeper and the other servants who had waited on him he entirely dispelled from their minds the idea that he was a picture-dealer.

"I suppose he is one of those foreign swells, after all," the footman who had served him said to the housekeeper, as he pocketed the *douceur* the Señor had given him; "there is plenty of 'em in London Society now."

He reached the London terminus late in the afternoon, and bade the cabman he hired drive him to the Hôtel Lepanto; but, before half the journey to that house was accomplished, the driver found himself suddenly called on by his fare to stop, and to turn round and follow another cab going in the opposite direction.

A hansom cab which had passed swiftly the one Señor Guffanta was in, a cab in which was seated a young man with a brown moustache, and on the roof of which was a portmanteau and a bundle of rugs.

"Quick!" the Señor said, speaking for the first time almost incoherent English; "follow that cab with the valise on the top. Quick, I say! I will pay you anything!"

"How can I be quick!" the man said with an oath, "when I can hardly turn my cab round? Which is the one you mean?"

"The one with the valise, I say, that passed just now. I will give you everything I have in my pockets if you catch it."

But it was no use. Before the cab could be turned and put in pursuit, the other one had disappeared round a corner into a short street, from which, ere Señor Guffanta's cab had reached it, it had again disappeared.

"Blood of my father!" the Señor said to himself in Spanish, "am I never to seize him?" Then he once more altered his directions to the cabman, and bade him drive to Occleve House.

He walked into the room in which he heard that Lord Penlyn and Mr. Stuart were seated, and the excitement visible upon his face told them that something had happened.

"I have seen him," he said, going through no formality of greeting; he was far too disturbed for that. "I have seen him once again, and once again I have lost him."

"Where have you seen him?" Stuart asked.

"Not at Occleve Chase, surely!" Penlyn exclaimed.

"No—here, in London! Not half-an-hour ago, in a cab. And I have missed him! He went too swiftly, and I lost sight of him."

"What will you do?" they both exclaimed.

"At present I do not know. I feel as though I shall go mad!" Then a moment after he said: "Give me the keys of the garden; at once, give them to me."

Penlyn took them from a drawer and gave them to Señor Guffanta, and he, bidding the others remain where they were, opened the door leading into the garden from the back of the house, and went out into it.

It was but a few minutes before he returned, but when he did so the bronze had left his face and he was deathly pale.

"Lord Penlyn," he said, biting his lips as he spoke, and clenching his hands until the nails penetrated the palms, "to whom have you given those keys during my absence?"

"To no one," Penlyn answered. "I promised you I would not let any one have them."

"You have given them to no one?" Guffanta said, while his eyes shone fiercely as he looked at the other. "To no one! To no one! Then will you tell me how the murderer of Walter Cundall has been in that garden within the last few hours?"

CHAPTER XVIII.

That night Guffanta stood in the library of what had once been Walter Cundall's house in Grosvenor Place, in the room in which the murdered man had spent hours of agony after he had learned that Ida Raughton's love was given to another; and to Mr. Stuart he told all that he knew. To Lord Penlyn's request, nay to his command, that he should tell him all, he paid no attention; indeed, he vouchsafed no words to him beyond those of suspicion and accusation.

"I know so much," he said, speaking in the calm, cold voice which had only once failed him—the time when he had discovered that the assassin had in some way obtained entrance to the deserted garden during his absence, "as to be able to say that you are not your brother's murderer. But, unless there is something very strange that as yet I do not know, that murderer is known to you, and you are shielding him from me."

"It is false!" Lord Penlyn said, advancing to him and standing boldly and defiantly before him. "As God hears me, I swear that it is false. And you *shall* tell me what you know, you shall justify your vile suspicions of me."

"Yes," the Señor replied, "I shall justify them, but not *to* you. Meanwhile, have a care that I do not prove you to be an accomplice in this murder. Have a care, I say!"

"I defy you and your accusations. And the law shall make you speak out plainly."

"I am about to speak out plainly, this very night. But I am not going to speak plainly to the man whose house affords a refuge to his brother's murderer."

Lord Penlyn sprang at him, as he heard these words fall from his lips, as he had once sprung at his own brother in the Park when that brother told him he was bearing a name not rightly his; and once more he felt himself in a grasp of iron, and powerless.

"Be careful!" Señor Guffanta said, as he hurled him back, "be careful, or I shall do you an injury."

Stuart had endeavoured to come between them, but before he could do so the short struggle was over, and then the Spaniard turned to him and said, "I must speak with you alone. Come with me," and, turning, left the room.

Before Stuart followed him he spoke to Penlyn, and said: "Do not take this too seriously to heart. This man is evidently under some delusion, if not as to the actual murderer, at least as to your connection with the crime. Perhaps, when he has told me what he knows, we shall find out where the error lies; and then he will ask your pardon for his suspicions."

"It is too awful!" Penlyn said, "too awful to be borne. And I can do nothing. I wish I could have killed him as he stood there falsely accusing me, but he is a giant in strength."

"Let me go to him now," Stuart said; "and do not think of his words. Remember, he, too, is excited at having seen the man again and missed him. And if he does not absolutely bind me to silence I will tell you all." Then he, also, went away. And that night, in Walter Cundall's library, Señor Guffanta told his story. Told it calmly and dispassionately, but with a fulness of detail that struck a chill to Stuart's heart.

"I had been but a few days in London," he said, "when I learnt by Walter's own hand—in the letter you have seen—that he was also here, and that I was to go and see him. I was eager to do so, and on the very night he was murdered, on that fatal Monday night, I set out to visit him. He had told me to come late, and knowing that he was a man much in the world, and also that, from living in Honduras, where the nights alone are cool, one rarely learns to go to bed early, I did go late; so late that the clocks were striking midnight as I reached his house. But, when I stood outside it, there was no light of any kind to be seen, only a faint glimmer from a lamp in the hall. 'He has gone to his bed,' I said to myself, 'and the house is closed for the night. Well, it is indeed late, I will come again.' And so I turned away, and, knowing that there was a road through your Park, though I had not gone by it, I determined to return that way."

"Through the Park—where he was murdered?" Stuart asked.

"Yes, by that way. But before I reached the gates, and when I was outside the Palace of your Queen, Buckingham Palace, the storm that had been threatening broke over me. *Caramba!* it was a storm to drown a man, a storm such as we see sometimes in the tropics, but which I had never thought to see here. It descended in vast sheets of water, it was impossible to stir without being instantaneously drenched to the skin, and so I sought shelter in a porch close at hand. There, seeing no one pass me but some poor half-drowned creature who looked as though the rain could make his misery no greater than it was, I waited and waited—I had no protection, no umbrella—and heard the quarters and half-hours, and the hours tolled by the clock. At last, as it was striking two, the storm almost ceased, and, leaving my shelter, I crossed the road and entered the Park."

"Yes!" Stuart said in a whisper.

"Yes, I entered the Park, and went on round the bend, and so, under the dripping trees, through what I have since learnt, is called the 'Mall.'"

"For God's sake, go on!" Stuart exclaimed.

"I had passed some short distance on my road meeting no living creature, when but a little distance ahead of me I saw two figures struggling, the figures of two men. Then I saw one fall, and the other—not seeing me, there were trees between us—passed swiftly by. But I saw him and his face, the face of a young man dressed as a peasant, or, as you say here, a workman; a young man with a brown moustache."

For a moment Señor Guffanta paused, and then he continued:

"I ran to the fallen man, and—it was Walter—dead! Stabbed to the heart! I called him by his name, I kissed him, and felt his breast; but he was dead! And then, in a moment, it came to my mind that it was not with him I had to do; it was with the murderer. I sprang to my feet, I left him there—there, dead in the mud and the water with which his blood now mingled—and, as quickly as I could go, I retraced my steps after that murderer. And God is good! I had wasted but two or three moments with my poor dead friend, and ere I again reached the gates of the Park I saw before me the figure of the man who had passed me under the trees. He was still walking swiftly, and once or twice he looked round, as though fearing he was followed. But I, who have tracked savage beasts to their lairs, and Indians to their haunts, knew how to track him. Keeping well behind him and at a fair distance, sometimes screening myself behind the pillar on a doorstep, and sometimes crossing the road, sometimes even letting myself fall back still farther, I followed him. At one time, when I first brought him into my sight again, it had been in my thoughts to spring upon him, and there at once to kill him or take him prisoner. And then I thought it best not to do so. We had moved far from the scene; who was to prove, how was I to prove that it was he who had done this deed, and not I? And there was blood upon my clothes and hands—it was plainly visible! I could see it myself! blood that had flown from Walter's dead heart on to me as I took him in my arms upon the ground. No, I said, I must follow him, I must know where he lives, then I will take fresh counsel with myself as to what I shall do. So I went on, still following him. And by this time the dawn was breaking! He went on and on, walking, perhaps, for half-an-hour or so, though it seemed far more to me; but at last he stopped, and I had now some difficulty in preventing him from seeing me. He had stopped at a gate in a wall, and with a key had quickly opened it."

"The gate of the garden of Occleve House!" Stuart exclaimed, quivering with excitement.

"Yes," the Señor answered, "the gate of the garden of Occleve House."

"My God!" the other said.

"Yes, it was that gate. And now I had to be careful. I was determined to see where he had gone to through that gate, what he was doing in that garden; but how to do it? If I looked through the railings he would see me, he would know he was discovered—he might even then be able to escape me! If I had had my pistol with me, I would have stood by the gate and looked at him through it, and then, if necessary, would have shot him dead. But I had it not; I had thought of no need for it when I left the hotel that night. I did not know what was before me when I went out. But I knew I must do something at once, and so, seeing that the street was empty and no creature stirring, I advanced near to the gate, stretched myself flat upon the *pavé*, and with my head upon the ground looked under the lowest part of the railings and saw—"

"What?" Stuart asked, interrupting him again in his excitement.

"A changed man, one different from him I had followed. Still a young man with a brown moustache, but a young man whose habit was that of a gentleman. He was dressed now in a dark, well-made suit, and with his hands he was rolling up the peasant dress I had seen him wear. Then he stooped over what seemed to be a hole, or declivity, near the wall and dropped the suit into it, and arranged the weeds and long grass above it, and then slowly he went to the house, and, taking again a key from his pocket, entered the door."

"What man could thus have had the entrance to the back of the house?" Stuart asked. "I am bewildered with horrible thoughts!"

"I also was bewildered, but I am now no longer so. I knew the man's face; now—to-day—I know for certain who he was. Within the last few days it flashed upon me, yet I doubted; but my doubts are satisfied. I only learned of

117

his existence ten days ago, or I should have suspected him before."

"Who was it?" Stuart said. "Tell me at once."

"Wait yet a moment, and listen to me. As I saw that man enter the house, a house that I, a stranger, could see was the mansion of some person of importance, it came to me, to my mind, that this was the owner, the master of that house, who had killed my friend. His reason for doing so I could not guess—it might have been for the love of a woman, or for hate, or about money—but that it was so I was confident. And I said to myself, 'So! you cannot escape me! I know your house, to-morrow I shall know your name, and, if in two or three days the police have not got you in their power—I will wait that while, for it is better they should take you than I—then I will kill you.' And I went away thinking thus; there was no need to watch more. I held him, for he could not escape I thought, in my hand."

"But it was not the owner of the house," Stuart said, "it was not Lord Penlyn who killed him. He was away at an hotel at the time."

"Yes, he was—though still it would be possible for him then to have entered his own house—but his was not the face of the man I had seen. I learnt that, to my amazement, when for the first time I stood before him. But, listen again! In the morning, at a restaurant, I found in a Directory, of which I had learnt the use, that that house was Occleve House, and that Lord Penlyn was the owner of it. And then my surprise was great, for only an hour or so before I had found that Occleve was the right name of Walter Cundall."

"You had learnt that?"

"When I lifted Walter in my arms in the Park, I felt against his breast a book half out of his pocket. The murderer had missed that! I took that book, for even in my haste and grief, I thought that in it might be something that would give me a clue. But what were really in it of importance were a certificate of his mother's marriage, another of his own birth, and a letter, years old, from her to him. They told me all, and, moreover they proved to me, as I then thought, that his murderer lived in the very house and bore the very name that by right seemed to be his."

"They were the certificates he showed to them on the morning he disclosed himself," Stuart said, "and he had not removed them from his pocket-book when he was killed!"

"Yes! that he showed to *them*; you have said it! It was to *two* of them that he showed those papers. And one was the friend of the other, he lived with and upon him, he dares not meet me face to face, he evades me! he, he is the murderer. He, Philip Smerdon!"

Stuart sprung to his feet.

"Philip Smerdon!" he exclaimed. "No, no! it cannot be!"

"It is, I say! It is he. Of all others, who but he could have done this deed? Who but he who crept back to Occleve House having in his pocket the keys whereby to enter it, who but he who shuns me because it has been told him that I knew the assassin's face! And on the very night that he is back in London, sleeping in that house, are not the clothes that might have led to his identification removed?"

Stuart paused a moment, deep in thought, and then he said: "It cannot be! On the day before the murder, in the morning, he left London for Occleve Chase. He must have been there when it was committed."

"Bah!" Guffanta said, with a shrug of his shoulders, "he did not leave London, he only made a pretence of doing so. All that day he, in his disguise, must have been engaged in tracking my poor friend, and at night he killed him." Then he paused a moment, and when he next spoke he asked a question.

"Where was he going when he left Occleve House this afternoon in the cab, and with his luggage?"

"He was going to join his father, he said," Stuart answered. "His father is ill and has been ordered abroad for his health, and, having recovered some money from his ruined business, he is going on the Continent, and Smerdon is going with him."

"And to what part of the Continent are they going?"

"I do not know, though he said something about the French coast, and afterwards, the Tyrol. Why do you ask?

"Why do I ask? Why? Because I must go also! I have to stand face to face with him, and be able to convince myself that either I have made some strange mistake, or that I am right."

"And—if you are right?"

"Then I have to take him to the nearest prison, or, if he resists, to kill him."

"You will do that?"

"I will do anything necessary to prevent him ever escaping me again."

They talked on into the night, and Señor Guffanta extracted from the other a promise that he would lend him any assistance in his power, and that, above all, he would say nothing to Lord Penlyn that, by being retold to Smerdon, should, if he were actually the murderer, help him to still longer escape.

"I promise you," Stuart said, "and the more willingly because I myself would give him up to justice if I were sure he is the man. But that, of course, I cannot be; it is you alone who can identify this cruel murderer. But, in one thing I *am* sure you are wrong."

"In what thing?"

"In thinking that Lord Penlyn is in the slightest way an accomplice, or suspects Smerdon at all. If he did so suspect him, I believe that he would himself cause him to be arrested, even though they are such friends."

"What motive would Smerdon have to kill Walter except to remove him from the other's path? Do you think he would have done it without consulting Lord Penlyn?"

"I am certain that if he did do it, as you think—"

"As I am as convinced as that we are sitting here!"

"Well, then I am certain that Lord Penlyn knows nothing of it. He is hasty and impetuous, but he is the soul of honour."

"Perhaps," Guffanta said; "it may be so. But it is not with him that I have to deal. It is with the man who struck the blow. And it is him I go to seek."

"How will you find him?"

"Through you. You will find out for me where he is gone with his father—if this is not a lie invented to aid his further escape—and you will let me know everything. Is it not so?"

"Yes," Stuart said; "I myself swore that I would find the murderer if I could; but, as I cannot do that, I will endeavour to help you to do so. How shall I communicate with you?"

"Write, or come to the 'Hôtel Lepanto.' And when you once tell me where that man is, there I shall soon be afterwards. Even though he should go to the end of the world, I will follow him."

Then Señor Guffanta went back to his hotel, and told Diaz Zarates that he should soon be leaving his house.

"I have to make a little tour upon the Continent, and I may go at any moment."

"On a tour of pleasure, Señor?" the landlord asked.

"No! on a voyage of importance!"

And three days afterwards he went. A letter had come to him from Stuart saying:

"*S.* has really gone with his father. He has left London for Paris on the way to Switzerland. They are to pass the summer at some mountain resort, but the place is not yet decided on. At first they will be at Berne. If you meet, for God's sake be careful, and make no mistake."

"Yes!" Señor Guffanta muttered to himself as he packed his portmanteau, and prepared to catch the night mail to Paris. "Yes, I will be careful, very careful! And I will make no mistake!"

CHAPTER XIX.

The summer began to wane, and as August drew to a close the world of London at large forgot the murder of Walter Cundall.

It forgot it because it had so many other things to think about, because it had its garden parties and fêtes, and Henley and Goodwood; and because, after that, the exodus set in, and the Continent, Scotland, and Cowes, as well as all the other seaside resorts, claimed its attention. It is true one incident had come to light which had given a fillip to the dying curiosity of the world and society, but even that had scarcely tended to rouse fresh interest in the crime. This incident was the discovery that Lord Penlyn was the heir to all of the dead man's vast wealth. The news had come out gradually through different channels, and it had set people talking; but even then—at this advanced state of the London season—it had scarcely aroused more than a passing flutter of excitement. And society explained even this fact to its own satisfaction— perhaps because it had, by now, found so many other things of more immediate, and of fresher, interest. Cundall had been, it said, a man of superbly generous impulses, one who seemed to delight in doing acts of munificence that other men would never dream of; what more natural a thing for him to do than to leave his great wealth to the very man who had won the woman he had sought for his wife? Was it not at once a splendid piece of magnanimity, a glorious example of how one might heap coals of fire on those who thwarted us—was it not a truly noble way of retaliating upon the woman he loved, but who had no love for him? She would, through his bequest to her husband that was to be, become enormously rich, but she could never enjoy the vastness of those riches without remembering whence they came; every incident in her life would serve to remind her of him.

So, instead of seeing any cause for suspicion in the will of Walter Cundall, the world only saw in it a magnificently generous action, a splendidly noble retaliation. For it never took the trouble to learn the date of the will, but supposed that it had been made on the day after he had discovered that Ida Raughton had promised herself to another.

To those more directly interested in the murder and in the discovery of the assassin, the passing summer seemed to bring but little promise of success. Lord Penlyn knew that Señor Guffanta had left London, but beyond that he did not know what had become of him, nor whether it was the business of Don Rodriguez, or pleasure, or the search for the murderer that had taken him away. Stuart, who still believed him innocent of the slightest participation or knowledge of the crime, yet did not feel inclined to give him the least information as to the Señor's movements, fearing that, if Smerdon was the man—of which, as yet, he by no means felt positive—he might learn that he was being pursued; and so contented himself with saying as little as possible. As to Dobson, he had now come to the conclusion that the "Signor," as he always called him, was an arrant humbug, and really knew no more about the murder than he did himself. And as the detective had already received a handsome sum of money from Lord Penlyn for his services, such as they were, and as he had at the present moment what he called "one or two other good little jobs on," he gradually devoted himself to these matters, and the murder of Mr. Cundall ceased to entirely occupy his efforts. Though, as he was a man who did his duty to the best of his ability, he still kept one of his subordinates looking about and making inquiries in various places where he thought information might be obtained. But the information, as he confessed, was very long in coming.

From Señor Guffanta Stuart had heard more than once during his absence, which had now extended to three weeks, but the letters he received contained nothing but accounts of his failure to come upon the suspected man. In Paris, the Señor wrote, he had been absolutely unable to find any person of the name of Smerdon, though he had tried everything in his power to do so. He had pored daily over *Galignani* and other papers that contained the lists of strangers who arrived in the French capital, he had personally inspected the visitors' books in every hotel likely to be patronised by English people of good social position; but all to no effect. Then, determined, if his man was there, not to miss him, he had applied to the particular *bureau* of police at the Préfecture, where are kept, according to French law, the lists furnished weekly by every hotel-keeper and lodging-house keeper of their guests and tenants, both old and new; and these, being shown him, he had carefully searched, and still he had failed. He was induced to think, he wrote Stuart, that Smerdon, either alone or with his family (if he really had them with him) must have changed his route, or his destination, at the last moment. Or, perhaps they had travelled by Brussels and the Rhine to Switzerland, or passed through Paris from one station to the other without stopping, or they might have gone by the way of Rheims and Delle from Calais to Basle. Could Mr. Stuart, he asked, obtain any further information from Lord Penlyn as to the whereabouts of the man whose face he wished to see, for if he could not, he did not know where to look for him.

In answer to this, Stuart wrote back that no letter had come from Smerdon since the day he left Occleve House, the day on which the Señor had seen the murderer in the cab, but that he had little doubt that the former was now in Switzerland. "Why," he wrote, "since you are determined to make yourself sure about Smerdon's identity with the man you saw kill our friend, do you not go on into Switzerland? There you could have but little difficulty in finding him, for printed lists of the visitors to almost every resort, small or large, are published daily or weekly. Any bookseller would procure you the *Fremdenblatts* and *Listes des Étrangers*, and if you could only find his name at one spot, you would be sure to catch him up at last. When a traveller leaves an hotel in Switzerland, the train, or boat, or diligence is a sure indication of what district he is changing to, and any intelligent porter or servant will in all probability be able to remember any person you can describe fairly accurately."

To this a letter came back from Guffanta, saying that he acknowledged the reason of Mr. Stuart's remarks, and that he would waste no more time in Paris but would at once set out for Switzerland. "Only," he wrote, in his usual grave and studied style, "you must pardon me for what I am now going to say, and for what I am going to ask. It is for money. I have exhausted my store, which was not great when I arrived in England, and which has only been increased by a small draft on Don Rodriguez's London banker. I have enough to take me to Switzerland I find, but not enough to carry me into the heart of the country. Will you please send me some to the Poste Restante, at Basle? I will repay it some day, and be sure that I shall eventually gain the object we both desire in our hearts."

For answer to this, Stuart put a fifty-pound note in a registered letter, and forwarded it to the address Guffanta had given him. Then, when it had been acknowledged by the latter, he heard no more from him for some time.

During this period Lord Penlyn had been absent from town. He had received from Sir Paul Raughton, at the time when the Señor was about to leave London, a letter telling him that Ida was much better, and that he thought that Penlyn might see her if he went down to Belmont. Sir Paul had faithfully delivered the message given him, and to Ida this, he said, had been the best medicine. At first she would scarcely believe it possible that her lover would ever again see her or speak of love to her; but, when she learnt that not only was he anxious to do this, but that it was he himself whom he considered in the wrong, and that, instead of extending his pardon to her, he was anxious to sue for hers, the colour came back to her cheek and the smile to her eyes and lips.

"Oh, papa!" she said, as she sat up one day in her boudoir and nestled close to him, "oh, papa, how could I ever think so ill of him, of him who is everything that is good and noble? How wicked I have been! How wicked and unjust!"

"Of course!" Sir Paul exclaimed, "that is just the kind of thing a woman always does say. She quarrels with the man she loves, and then, just because he wants to make up the quarrel as much as she does, she thinks she has been in the wrong. And after all, mind you, Ida, although I don't believe that Penlyn had any more to do with the murder than I had—"

"No, papa!" speaking firmly.

"Still he does not come out of the affair with flying colours. He never moved hand nor foot to find out who really had done it, and he kept the secret of poor Cundall being his brother from me. He oughtn't to have done that!"

Sir Paul did feel himself aggrieved at this. He thought that, as Ida's father, he should have been told everything bearing upon the connection between the two men, and he considered that there had been some intention to deceive him on the part of Penlyn. In his joy at the prospect of his daughter's renewed happiness he was very willing to forgive Penlyn, but still he could not help mentioning his errors, as he considered them.

"Remember the letter from his brother, papa! It contained his solemn injunctions—rendered doubly solemn by the awful fate that overtook him on the very night he wrote them! How could he confide the secret to any one after that?"

Her father made no answer to this question, not knowing what to say. After all, he acknowledged that had he been made the custodian of such a secret, had he had such solemn injunctions laid on him as Cundall had laid on his brother, he would have tried to keep them equally well. Honestly, he could not tell himself that Penlyn should have broken the solemn command imposed upon him; the command issued by a man who, as he gave it, was standing at the gate of the grave.

So, when Penlyn paid his next visit to Belmont, there was a very different meeting between him and its inmates from the meetings that had gone before.

Sir Paul took him by the hand, and told him that he was sincerely happy in knowing that once more he and Ida were thoroughly united, and then he went into her. Not a moment elapsed before she was folded to his heart and he had kissed her again and again, not a moment before she was beseeching him to forgive her for the injurious thoughts and suspicions she had let come into her mind.

"Hush, Ida hush, my darling!" he said, as he tried to soothe her; "it is not you who should ask for forgiveness, but I. Not because I kept my brother's secret from you, but because of the brutal way in which I cast you off, simply for your doubting me for one moment. Oh, Ida, my own, say that you forgive me."

"I have nothing to forgive," she said; "the fault was mine. I should never have doubted you."

And so once more they were united, united never more to part. And since everything was now known to Ida, her future husband was able to talk freely to her, to tell her other things that had transpired of late, and especially of, what seemed to him, the strange behaviour of the Señor, and the accusation he had brought against him of shielding the murderer in his house.

"Oh, Gervase!" Ida exclaimed, "why is it that every one should be so unjust to you? Was it not enough that I should have suspected you—though only for a moment in my grief and delirium—without this man doing so in another manner. It is monstrous, monstrous!"

"Your suspicions," he answered, "were natural enough. You had had your mind disturbed by that strange dream, and, when you heard of my relationship to Cundall, it was natural that your thoughts should take the turn they did. But I cannot understand Guffanta, nor what he means."

He had recognised many times during the estrangement between him and Ida that her temporary suspicion of him was natural enough, and that—being no heroine of romance, but only a straightforward English girl, with a strange delusion as to having seen the assassin in her dream—it was not strange she should have doubted him; but for Guffanta's accusation he could find no reason. Over and over again he had asked himself whom it could be that he suspected? and again and again he had failed to find an answer. On that fatal night there had been no one sleeping in Occleve House but the servants, no one who could have gained admission to it; yet the Señor had charged him with sheltering the man who had done the deed, both on that night and afterwards.

"Can he not be made to speak out openly?" Ida asked. "Can he not be made to say who the person was whose face he saw? Why do you not force him to do so?"

"I have seen nothing of him since the night he accused me of protecting the murderer, and he has left the hotel he was staying at."

"Where is he gone?" Ida asked.

"No one seems to know, though Stuart says he fancies he is still looking for the murderer. I pray God he may find him."

"And I too!" Ida said.

After this meeting, Penlyn acceded to the request of Sir Paul and his future wife that he should stay at Belmont for some time, and he took up his abode there with them. His valet came down from town, bringing with him all things necessary for a stay in the country, and then Ida passed happier days in the society of her lover than she had ever yet enjoyed. They spent their mornings together sitting under the firs upon the lawn, they drove together—for she was still too weak to ride in the afternoons; and in the evenings Sir Paul would join them. Their marriage had been postponed for two months in consequence of Ida's ill health, but they knew that by the end of October they would be happy, and so they bore the delay without repining. One thing alone chastened their happiness—the memory of the dead man, and the knowledge that his murderer had not been brought to justice.

"I swore upon his grave to avenge him," Penlyn said, "and I have done nothing, can do nothing. If any one ever avenges him it will be Señor Guffanta, and I sometimes doubt if he will be able to do so. It seems a poor termination to the vows I took."

"Perhaps it is but a natural one," Ida answered. "It is only in romances, and in some few cases of real life, that a murder planned as this one must have been is punished. Yet, so long as we live, we will pray that some day his wicked assassin may be discovered."

"Do you still think," Penlyn asked, "that the figure which you saw in your dream was known to you in actual life? Do you think that if the murderer is ever found you will remember that you have known him?"

"It was a dream," she answered, "only a dream! Yet it made a strange impression on me. You know that I also said that, if once I could remember to what man in actual life that figure bore a resemblance, I would have his every action of the past and present closely scrutinised; yet I, too, can do nothing. Even though I could identify some living person with that figure, what could I, a woman, do?"

"Nothing, darling," her lover answered her, "we can neither of us do anything. If Guffanta cannot find him, we must be content to leave his punishment to heaven."

So, gradually, they came to think that never in this world would Walter Cundall's death be avenged, and gradually their thoughts turned to other things, to the happy life that seemed before them, and to the way in which that life should be spent. Under the fir trees they would sit and plan how the vast fortune that the dead man had left should best be laid out, how an almshouse bearing his name should be erected at Occleve Chase, and how a large charity, also in his name, should be endowed in London. And even then, they knew that but a drop of his wealth would be spent; it would necessitate unceasing thought upon their part to gradually get it all distributed in a manner that should do good to others.

"He was the essence of charity and generosity," Penlyn said, "it shall be by a charitable and generous disposal of his wealth that we will honour his memory."

They were seated on their usual bench one evening, still making their plans, when they saw one of Sir Paul's footmen coming towards them and bringing the usual batch of papers and letters. It was the time at which the post generally came in, and they had made a habit of having their correspondence brought to them there, and of passing the half-hour before dinner in reading their letters. The man handed several to Lord Penlyn and one to Ida, and they began to peruse them. Those to Penlyn were ordinary ones and did not take long in the reading, and he was about to turn round and ask Ida if hers were of any importance, when he was startled by a sound from her lips,—a sound that was half a gasp and half a moan. As he looked at her, he saw that she had sunk back against the wooden rail of the garden seat, and that she was deathly pale. The letter she had received, and the envelope bearing the green stamp of Switzerland, had fallen at her feet.

"Ida! my dearest! what is it?" he exclaimed, as he bent towards her and placed his arm round her. "Ida! have you had bad news, have you—?"

"The dream," she moaned, "the dream! Oh, God!"

"What dream?" he said, while a sweat of horror, of undefined, unknown horror broke out upon his forehead. "What dream?"

"The letter! Read the letter!" she answered, while in her eyes was a look he had once seen before—the far-away look that had been there when he first spoke to her of his brother's murder.

He stooped and picked up the letter—picked it up and read it hurriedly; and then he, too, let it fall again and leaned back against the seat.

"Philip Smerdon my brother's murderer!" he exclaimed. "Philip Smerdon, my friend, an assassin! The self-accused, the self-avowed murderer of Walter Cundall! Ida," he said, turning to her, "is *his* the figure in your dream?"

"Yes," she wailed. "Yes! I recognise it now."

CHAPTER XX.

The Schwarzweiss Pass, leading from the south-east of Switzerland to Italy, is one well known to mountaineers, because of the rapid manner in which they can cross from one country to another, and also because of the magnificent views that it presents to the traveller. Moreover, it offers to them a choice either of making a passage over the snow-clad mountains that rise above it, and across the great Schwarzweiss glacier, or of keeping to the path that, while rising to the height at some places of 10,000 feet, is, except at the summit, perfectly passable in good weather. It is true that he who, even while on the path, should turn giddy, or walk carelessly, would risk his life, for though above him only are the vast white "horns" and "Piz," below him there are still the ravines through which run the boiling torrents known respectively as the "Schwarz" and the "Weiss" rivers—rivers that carry with them huge boulder stones and pine-trees wrenched from their roots; dry slopes that fall hundreds of feet down into the valley below; and also the Klein (or little) Schwarzweiss glacier, a name so given it, not because of its smallness—for it is two miles long, and in one place, half-a-mile across—but to distinguish it from the Gross-Schwarzweiss glacier that hangs above on the other side of the pass.

It is a lonely and grim road, a road in which no bird is heard or seen from the time that the village of St. Christoph is left behind on the Swiss side until the village of Santa Madre is reached on the Italian side; a road that winds at first, and at last, through fir-woods and pine-trees, but that in the middle is nothing but a path, cut in some parts and blasted in others, along the granite sides of the rocks, and hanging in many places above the valley far below. Patches of snow and pieces of rock that have fallen from above, alone relieve the view on the side of the path; on the opposite side of the ravine is nothing but a huge wall of granite that holds no snow, so slippery is it; but above which hangs, white and gray, like the face of a corpse, the glacier from which the pass derives its name.

A lonely and grim road even in the daytime, when a few rays of sunshine manage to penetrate it at midday, when occasionally a party of tourists may be met with, and when sometimes the voice of a goatherd calling his flocks rises from the valley below; but lonelier and more grim, and more black and impenetrable at night, and rarely or ever then trod by human foot. For he who should attempt the passage of the Schwarzweiss Pass at night, unless there were a brilliant moon to light him through its most dangerous parts, would take his life in his own hands.

Yet, on an August night of the year in which this tale is told, and when there was a moon that, being near its full, consequently rose late and shone till nearly daylight, a man was making his way across this pass to Italy.

Midnight was close at hand as, with weary steps, he descended a rough-hewn path in the rock—a path which, for safety, had a rude handrail of iron attached to the side from which it was cut—and reached a small plateau, the size, perhaps, of an ordinary room, and from which again the path went on. From this plateau shelved down, for a hundred feet or more, an almost perpendicular moraine, or glacier bed, and at the foot of this lay the Klein-Schwarzweiss, with its crevasses glistening in the moonlight; for the moon had topped even the great mountains above by now, and lighted up the pass. It was evidently considered a dangerous part of the route, since between the edge of the plateau and the side of the moraine a wooden railing had been erected, consisting of two short upright posts and a long cross one. As the man reached this plateau, holding to the rail with one hand, while with the other he used his alpenstock as a walking-stick, he perceived a stone—it may have been placed there for the purpose—large enough for a seat; and taking off his knapsack wearily, he sat down upon it.

"Time presses," he muttered to himself, "yet I must rest. Otherwise I shall not be at Santa Madre by eight o'clock to-morrow. I can go no farther without a rest."

There is an indefinite feeling of awfulness in being alone at night amongst the mountains, in knowing and feeling that for miles around there is no other creature in these vast, cold solitudes but ourselves: and this man had that feeling now.

"How still—how awful this pass is!" he said to himself, "with no sound but the creaking of that glacier below—with no human being here but me. Yet, I should be glad I am alone."

At this moment a few stones in the moraine slipped and fell into the glacier, and the man started at the distinct sound they made in that wilderness of silence. Then, as he sat there gazing up at the moon and the snow above him, he continued his meditations.

"It is best," he thought, "that the poor old mother did not know when I said 'good-bye' to her this afternoon, and she bade me come back soon, that I should never come back, that I had a farther destination than Italy before me; best that my father did not know that we should never meet again. Never! never! Ah, God! it is a long word."

"Yet it must be done," he went on. "If I want to drag this miserable life out, I must do it elsewhere than in England. That sleuth-hound will surely find me there; it is possible that he will even track me to the antipodes. Yet, if I were sure that he is lying about—having seen my face before, I would go back and brave him. Where did he ever see it?—where?—where? To my knowledge I have never seen him."

He rose and walked to the railing above the moraine, and looked down at the glacier, and listened to the cracking made by the seracs. "I might make an end of it now," he thought. "If I threw myself down there, it would be looked upon as an ordinary Alpine accident. But, no! that is the coward's resource. I have blasted my life for ever by one foul deed; let me endure it as a reparation for my crime. But what is my future to be? Am I to live a miserable existence for years in some distant country, frightened at every strange face, dreading to read every newspaper that reaches me for fear that I shall see myself denounced in it, and never knowing a moment's peace or tranquillity? Ah, Gervase! I wonder what you would say if you knew that, for your sake, I have sacrificed every hope of happiness in this world and all my chances of salvation in the next." He went back to the big stone after uttering these thoughts and sat down wearily upon it. "If I could know that that Spaniard was baffled at last and had lost all track of me, I could make my arrangements more calmly for leaving Europe, might even look forward to returning to England some day, and spending my life there while expiating my crime. But, while I know nothing, I must go on and on till at last I reach some place where I may feel safe."

He looked at his watch as he spoke to himself, and saw that the night was passing. "Another five minutes' rest," he said, "and I will start again across the pass."

As he sat there, taking those last five minutes of rest, it seemed to him that there was some other slight sound breaking the stillness of the night, something else besides the occasional cracking noise made by the glacier below and the subdued roar of the torrents in the valley. A light, regular sound, that nowhere else but in a solitude like this would, perhaps, be heard, but that here was perfectly distinct. It came nearer and nearer, and once, as it approached, some small stones were dislodged and rattled down from above, and fell with a plunge on to the glacier below: and then, as it came closer, he knew that it was made by the footsteps of a man. And, looking up, he saw a human figure descending the path to the plateau by which he had come, and standing out clearly defined against the moonlight.

"It is some guide going home," he said to himself, "or starting out upon an early ascent. How firmly he descends the path."

The man advanced, and he watched him curiously, noticing the easy way in which he came down the rough-hewn steps, scarcely touching the handrail or using the heavy-pointed stick he carried in place of the usual alpenstock. And he noticed that, besides his knapsack, he carried the heavy coil of rope that guides use in their ascents.

At last the new comer reached the plateau, and, as he took the last two or three steps that led on to it, he saw that there was another man upon it, and stopped. Stopped to gaze for one moment at the previous occupant, and then to advance towards him and to stand towering above him as he sat upon the boulder-stone.

"You are Philip Smerdon," he said in a voice that sounded deep and hollow in the other's ear.

Utterly astonished, and with another feeling that was not all astonishment, Smerdon rose and stood before him and said:

"I do not know of what importance my name can be to you."

"Your name is of no importance, but you are of the greatest to me. When I tell you *my* name you will understand why. It is Miguel Guffanta."

"Guffanta!" Smerdon exclaimed, "Guffanta!"

"Yes! the friend of Walter Cundall."

"What do you want with me?" the other asked, but as he asked he knew the answer that would come from the man before him.

"But one thing now, though ten minutes ago I wanted more. I wanted to see, then, if the man whom I sought for in London and at Occleve Chase, whom I have followed from place to place till I have found him here, was the same man I saw stab my friend to death in—"

"You saw it?"

"Yes, I saw it. And you are the man who did it!"

"It is false!"

"It is true! Do you dare to tell me I lie, you, a— Bah! Why should I cross words with a murderer—a thief!"

"I am no thief!" Smerdon said, his anger rising at this opprobrious term, even as he felt his guilt proclaimed.

"You are! You stole his watch and money because you thought to make his murder appear a common one. And so it was! You slew him because you feared he would dispossess your master of what he unrighteously held, because you thought that you would lose your place."

"Again I say it is false! I had no thought of self! I killed him—yes, I!—because I loved my friend, my master as you term him, because he threatened to come between him and the woman he loved. Had I known of Walter Cundall's noble nature, as I knew of it afterwards, no power on earth could have induced me to do such a deed."

"It is infamy for such as you to speak of his nobility—but enough! Are you armed to-night, as you were on that night?"

"I have no arms about me. Why do you ask?"

"To tell you that no arms can avail you now. You must come with me."

"To where?"

"To the village prison at St. Christoph. There I will leave you until you can be taken to England."

For the first time since he had seen the avenger of Walter Cundall standing before him, Smerdon smiled bitterly.

"Señor Guffanta," he said, "you are very big and strong—it may well be stronger than I am. But you overrate your strength strangely if you think that any power you possess can make me go with you. I am a murderer—God help and pardon me! It is probable I shall be a double one before this night is over."

"You threaten me—you! You defy me!" Guffanta exclaimed, while his dark eyes gleamed ominously.

"Yes, I defy you! If my sin is to be punished, it shall not be by you, at least. Here, in this lonely place where for miles no other human creature is near, I defy you to do your worst. We are man to man; do you think I fear you?"

In a moment Guffanta had sprung at him, had seized him by the throat, and with the other arm had encircled his body.

"So be it," he hissed in Smerdon's ear, "it suits me better than a prolonged punishment of your crime would do."

For a moment they struggled locked together, and in that moment Smerdon knew that he was doomed; that he was about to expiate his crime. The long, sinewy hand of the Spaniard that was round his throat was choking him; his own blows fell upon the other's body harmlessly. And he was being dragged towards the edge of the moraine, already his back was against the wooden railing that alone stood between the plateau and destruction. He could, even at this moment, hear it creaking with his weight; it would break in another instant!

"Will you yield, assassin, villain?" Guffanta muttered.

"Never! Do your worst."

He felt one hand tighten round his throat more strongly, he felt the other arm of the Spaniard driving him back; in that moment of supreme agony he heard the breaking of the railing and felt it give under him, and then Guffanta's hands had loosed him, and, striking the moraine with his head, he fell down and down till he lay a senseless mass upon the white bosom of the glacier.

And Guffanta standing above, with his head bared to the stars and to the waning moon, exclaimed, as he lifted his hand to the heavens, "Walter, you are avenged."

The day dawned upon the plateau; a few struggling rays of the sun illuminated the great glacier above and turned its dead gray snow and ice into a pure, warm white, while the mists rolled away from the high mountains keeping watch above; and below on the smaller glacier, and at the edge of a yawning crevasse, lay the body of Philip Smerdon.

Two guides, proceeding over the pass to meet a party of mountain climbers, reached the plateau at dawn, and sitting down upon the stone to eat a piece of bread and take a draught of cold coffee, saw his knapsack lying beside it.

"What does it mean?" the one said to the other.

"It means death," his companion replied, "the railing is broken! Some one has fallen."

Slowly and carefully, and each holding to one of the upright posts, they peered over and down on to the glacier, and there they saw what was lying below. A whispered word sufficed, a direction given by one to the other, and these hardy mountaineers were descending the moraine, digging their sticks deeply into the stones, and gradually working their way skilfully to the glacier.

"Is he dead, Carl?" the one asked of his friend, who stooped over the prostrate form and felt his heart.

"No; he lives. Mein Gott! how has he ever fallen here without instant death? But he must die! See, his bones are all broken!" and as he spoke he lifted Smerdon's arm and touched one of his legs.

"What shall we do with him?" the other asked.

"We must remove him. Even though he die on the way, it is better than to leave him here. Let us take him to the house of Father Neümann. It is but to the foot of the glacier."

Very gently these men lifted him in their arms, though not so gently but that they wrung a groan of agony from him as they did so, and bore him down the glacier to where it entered the valley; and then, having handed him to the priest, who lived in what was little better than a hut, they left him.

Late that afternoon the dying man opened his eyes, and looked round the room in which he lay. At his bedside he saw a table with a Cross laid upon it, and at the window of the room an aged priest sat reading a Breviary. "Where am I?" he asked in English.

The priest rose and came to the bed, and then spoke to him in German. "My son," he said, "what want of yours can I supply?"

"Tell me where I am," Smerdon answered in the same language, "and how long I have to live."

"You are in my house, the house of the *Curé* of Sastratz. For the span of your life none can answer but God. But, my son, I should do ill if I did not tell you that your hours are numbered. The doctor from St. Christoph has seen you."

"Give me paper and ink—"

"My son, you cannot write, and—"

"I *will* write," Smerdon said faintly, "even though I die in the attempt."

The *Curé* felt his right arm, which was not broken like the other, and then he brought him paper and ink, and holding the former up on his Breviary before the dying man, he put the pen in his hand. And slowly and painfully, and with eyes that occasionally closed, Smerdon wrote:

"I am dying at the house of the *Curé* of Sastratz, near the Schwarzweiss Pass; from a fall. Tell Gervase that *I alone murdered Walter Crandall*. If he will come to me and I am still alive, I will tell him all.

"PHILIP SMERDON."

Then he put the letter in an envelope and addressed it to Ida Raughton. And ere he once more lapsed into unconsciousness, he asked the priest to write another for him to his mother, and to address it to an hotel at Zurich.

"They will be sent at once?" he asked faintly.

"Surely, my son."

CHAPTER XXI.

It was late on the evening of the fifth day after the letter had been sent to Ida Raughton, that a mule, bearing upon its back Lord Penlyn and escorted by a guide, stopped at the house of the *Curé* of Sastratz; The young man had travelled from London as fast as the expresses could carry him, and had come straight to the village lying at the entrance of the Schwarzweiss Pass, to find that from there he could only continue his journey on foot or by mule. He chose the latter as the swiftest and easiest course—for he was very tired and worn with travelling—and at last he arrived at his destination.

When the first feeling of horror had been upon him on reading the letter Smerdon had written, acknowledging that he was the murderer, he had told Ida Raughton that he would not go to see him even on his death-bed; that his revulsion of feeling would be such that he should be only able to curse him for his crime. But she, with that gentleness of heart that never failed her, pleaded so with him to have pity on the man who, however deep his sin, had sinned alone for him, that she induced him to go.

"Remember," she said, "that even though he has done this awful deed, he did it for your sake; it was not done to benefit himself. Bad and wicked as it was, at least that can be pleaded for him."

"Yes," her lover answered, "I see his reason now. He thought that Walter

135

had come between my happiness and me for ever, and in a moment of pity for me he did the deed. How little he knew me, if he thought I wished him dead!"

But even as he spoke he remembered that he had once cursed his brother, and had used the very words "I wish he were dead!" If it was upon this hasty expression that Smerdon had acted, then he, too, was a murderer.

He left Belmont an hour after the letter had arrived, and so, travelling as above described, stood outside Father Neümann's house on the night of the fifth day. The priest answered the door himself, and as he did so he put his finger upon his lip. "Are you the friend from England that is expected?" he asked.

"Yes," Penlyn said, speaking low in answer to the sign for silence. "He still lives?"

"He lives; but his hours draw to a close. Had you not come now you would not have found him alive."

"Let me see him at once."

"Come. His mother is with him."

He followed the *Curé* into a room sparsely furnished, and of unpolished pine-wood; a room on which there was no carpet and but little furniture; and there he saw the dying form of Philip Smerdon. Kneeling by the bedside, and praying while she sobbed bitterly, was a lady whom Lord Penlyn knew to be Smerdon's mother. She rose at his entrance, and brushed the tears from her eyes.

"You have come in time to see him die," she said, while her frame was convulsed with sobs. "He has been expecting you. He said he could not pass away until he had seen you."

Penlyn said some words of consolation to her, and then he asked:

"Is he conscious?"

The poor mother leant over the bed and spoke to him, and he opened his eyes.

"Your friend has come, Philip," she said.

A light came into his eyes as he saw Penlyn standing before him, and then in a hollow voice he asked her to leave them alone.

"I have something to say to him," he said; "and the time is short."

"Yes," he said when she was gone, and speaking faintly in answer to Penlyn, who said he had come as quickly as possible; "yes, I know it. I expected you. And now that you are here can you bring yourself to say that you forgive me?"

For one moment the other hesitated, then he said: "I forgive you. May God do so likewise."

"Ah! that is it—it is that that makes death terrible! But listen! I must speak at once, I have but a short time more. This is my last hour, I feel it, I know it."

"Do not distress yourself with speaking. Do not think of it now."

"Not think of it! When have I ever forgotten it! Come closer, listen. I thought he had come between you and Miss Raughton for ever. I never dreamed of the magnanimity he showed in that letter. Then I determined to kill him—I thought I could do it without it being known. I did not go to the 'Chase' on that morning, but, instead, tracked him from one place to another, disguised in a suit of workman's clothes that I had bought some time ago for a fancy dress ball. I thought he would never leave his club that night; but at last he came out, and then—then—God! I grow weaker!—I did it."

Penlyn buried his head in his hands as he listened to this recital, and once he made a sign as though begging Smerdon to stop, but he did not heed him.

"I had with me a dagger I bought at Tunis, a long, sharp knife of the kind used by the Arabs, and I loosened it from its sheath as we entered the Park, he walking a few steps ahead of me, and, evidently, thinking deeply. Between the lamps I quickened my pace and passed him, and then, turning round suddenly, I seized him by the coat and stabbed him to the heart. It was but the work of a moment and he fell instantly, exclaiming only as he did so, 'Murderer!' Then to give it the appearance of a murder committed for theft, I stooped over him and wrenched his watch away, and as I took it I saw that he was dead. The watch is at Occleve Chase, in the lowest drawer of my writing-desk."

"Tell me no more," Penlyn said, "tell me no more."

"There is no more—only this, that I am glad to die. My life has been a curse since that day, I am thankful it is at an end. Had Guffanta not hurled me on to the glacier below, I think I must have taken it with my own hands."

"Guffanta!" Penlyn exclaimed, "is it he then who has done this?"

"It is he! He followed me from England here—in some strange way he was a witness to the murder—we met upon the pass and fought, he taxing me with being a murderer and a thief, and—and—ah! this is the end!"

His eyes closed, and Penlyn saw that his last moment was at hand. He called gently to Mrs. Smerdon, and she came in, and throwing herself by the side of the bed, took his hand and kissed it as she wept. The *Curé* entered at the same time and bent over him, and taking the Crucifix from his side, held it up before his eyes. Once they were fixed upon Penlyn with an imploring glance, and once they rested on his mother, and then they closed for ever.

"He is dead!" the priest said, "let us pray for the repose of his soul."

It was a few days afterwards that Ida Raughton, when walking up and down the paths at Belmont, heard the sound of carriage-wheels in the road outside, and knew that her lover was coming back to her. He had written from Switzerland saying that Smerdon was dead, and that he should wait to see him buried in the churchyard of St. Christoph—where many other English lay who had perished in the mountains—and he had that morning telegraphed from Paris to tell her that he was coming by the mail, and should be with her in the evening.

She walked swiftly to the house to meet him, but before she could reach it, he had come through the French windows of the morning-room, and advanced towards her.

"You have heard that he is dead, Ida?" he said, when he had kissed her, "it only remains for me to tell you that he died penitent and regretting his crime. It had weighed heavily upon him, and he was glad to go."

"And you forgave him, Gervase?" she asked.

"Yes. I forgave him. I could not but remember—as I saw him stretched there crushed and dying—that, though he had robbed me of a brother whom I must have come to love, he had sinned for me. Yes, if forgiveness belonged to me, I forgave him."

"Until we meet that brother in another world, Gervase, we have nothing but his memory to cherish. We must never forget his noble character."

"It shall be my constant thought," Penlyn answered, "to shape my life to what he would have wished it to be. And, Ida, so long as I live, his memory shall be second only in my heart to your own sweet self. Come, darling, it is growing late let us go in."

THE END.

Lightning Source UK Ltd.
Milton Keynes UK
UKHW042011060820
367798UK00002BA/463